MW01032022

LOVERBOY

BROTHERHOOD PROTECTORS WORLD

LEANNE TYLER

Twisted Page Press LLC

BROTHERHOOD PROTECTORS

ORIGINAL SERIES BY ELLE JAMES

To Ari, for believing I could finish this one when it looked like the story wasn't going to come.

CHAPTER 1

"CARLY, I'm thinking about biting a worm tonight. You game?" Jules Gentry held a breath, almost afraid her newly divorced friend would back down. It had taken Carly Porter, uh Manning, two long years to shed her controlling ex-husband in court.

"Depends on who, when, and where." Carly's eager come back surprised her.

"That's my girl! Simone and Colleen will pick you up. I'll catch the 'L' and meet you at the Pied Piper. See you in about thirty?"

"See you then."

"Oh and Carly, don't forget to wear the outfit we bought you."

There was a groan on the other end of the line before it went dead. Jules chuckled, placing her phone in the cradle before going to freshen up her makeup and head out the door. She just hoped

Simone's flight from DC hadn't been delayed or it would throw their plans off for tonight.

Jules needed a night out as much as Carly did. All the budget cuts that her youth center was going through right now, plus the endless meetings she'd been sitting through about said cuts had gotten them nowhere. In the end, they'd learned another imperative program was being dropped due to additional slashes to their funding and it all was ripping her heart out.

Her life's work was centered on the kids at this Chicago youth center and she really didn't know where they'd be if it were to close. These youth deserved better, way better than the officials were dishing out. It seemed every year the center went through another round of cutbacks. And this year was threatening to shut the doors.

She slipped her spring cerulean blue linen blazer on and picked up the white gift bag with pink tissue for Carly. A little something to celebrate her friend's new-found freedom from that control freak attorney she married seven years ago. Jules had seen the signs when the two were dating, but she'd been fresh out of college and wasn't sure if she was seeing the truth or imagining everyone she met had issues brought up in her psychology lectures.

Bless the judge who'd signed the divorce decree, finally seeing through Justin Porter and his overpriced divorce lawyer's stall tactics, setting Carly free from that nightmare of a marriage. Jules refused to let any man weight her down with that chain.

Leaving her apartment, she walked the few blocks to the 'L' and caught the train to the waterfront where she would meet her friends at the bar for a little rest, relaxation, and celebration. As the metro car zipped along the rails, Jules tried to put all the cares of the week behind her. It was time to focus on having fun, but every stop where a teen got on or off reminded her of the kids at her youth center. She couldn't stop wondering where they would end up if the center's programs were cut or the center itself were to close for good.

She didn't worry about herself so much. She could find a new job. It might take time, but she had savings. She lived frugally for the most part. She'd not taken on college loans so she wasn't in debt. Her grades had been good enough that she'd gotten her education on scholarships and grants. She might have to leave the area and her friends, but that would be the least of her worries right now.

Finally the 'L' came to her stop and she got off, walking the two blocks to the Pied Piper and taking in the early sultry summer heat.

She was the first to arrive so she ordered herself her favorite single-malt on the rocks and found a table for the four of them, next to the juke box Colleen always liked to hang around. It was also close to the dance area to satisfy Simone's free spirit. Jules settled in a chair so she could easily see the door and watch for her friends.

Since Carly rarely joined them on their girl's night out while she was married, Jules didn't know what Carly preferred in drink, music or seating. Tonight would be a first time for her to join them. She propped her feet up and leaned back in the chair, relaxing as she sipped her drink, letting the tension slowly leave her body until she saw her friends come through the door.

"Let this party get started," Simone called raising her arms in the air, a tiger print gift bag in one hand as she made her way between the tables.

Colleen carried a small gift bag as well and Carly followed with her large black purse that looked like she was prepared to spend the night elsewhere.

Jules felt her brow arch despite herself. This was exactly what they wanted for Carly, but she truly questioned whether their friend was really ready to go for it. She didn't want Carly doing anything she wasn't up for just to please them. That could spell disaster.

Jules got up and hugged Carly. "Let's get you a drink. What's your poison?"

Carly shrugged. "You said earlier you wanted to bite a worm. Doesn't that come with tequila?"

"It does indeed." Jules led her to the bar and order two shots of tequila. They downed the shots together.

"Holy mother," Carly gasped, sitting the glass back on the bar.

Jules chuckled, sat her glass down as well and sauntered back to her table and the single-malt scotch she'd left.

"Hit me again," she heard Carly say.

"Woohoo, that's the spirit!" Her friend Simone called from the nearby eight by eight stage area where she danced with the chrome pole. Her reddish-brown hair shimmered in the overhead spotlights.

Simone was already drawing attention as she shimmied against the pole, causing her spring dress to rise higher and higher with each move, showing off her long legs. She had a tiny waist, nice chest, and creamy skin tone to boot. A real beauty, and men had trouble not watching her when she walked into the room.

As expected, Colleen was dressed in a sedate skirt and blouse, swaying to the music by the jukebox, her blonde ponytail bobbed. For the two to be so close, they were polar opposites in personalities. But then, the four of them were an eclectic bunch.

Jules once again lounged at their table, her feet propped up, keeping a conscious eye on Carly.

"You guys look like a hair color commercial," Carly laughed.

"Look who's talking." Jules gestured with her drink. "You're the one who looks like something out of a Victoria's Secret catalog."

"What? I'm perfectly covered. Besides, you all picked it out." Carly reached a hand to her shoulder length honey-blonde hair and smoothed the imaginary flyaway strands back into place. The edges of her light-weight faux leather jacket pulled apart, revealing a white clinging tank top that showed off her flat tummy. The ensemble was finished with matching black short shorts that covered all the essentials and did marvelous things for her legs. As if they weren't long enough, the black studded, open toe, mid-ankle boots she wore added three more inches to her height. Simone had said the outfit had screamed 'take me home tonight', but they hadn't told Carly that.

Simone left the pole and danced over to the bar, looking Carly in the eye. "The whole point of this evening is to get you out of your comfort zone. You're the one that wanted a change in your life. We wanted it to be a liberation now that you're officially divorced from that control freak Justin Porter."

Carly downed the next shot of tequila and set the glass back on the bar. "Another one, bartender."

Colleen rushed over and reached for Carly's hand. "Pace yourself and don't forget to drink water. You don't want to find yourself flat on the floor," she warned with a sweet smile, leading her back to their table.

Simone followed with a tray containing a pitcher of water and the next round of drinks, which they toasted to Carly and her newfound freedom.

When the next song began to play, Jules removed her blazer, got to her feet and danced with Colleen and Simone. They urged Carly to join them, but she refused, deciding to sip water instead. A few frat boys from the University of Chicago joined them and they danced hard. Jules forgot about her worries. She even forgot about keeping an eye on Carly until she looked out at the table and noticed her friend was no longer sitting there.

"What's wrong?" the guy she was dancing with asked.

"Nothing. Just checking on a friend."

He nodded and pulled her closer as the song changed into a slower rhythm.

Jules didn't particularly like his assumption that she was okay with him getting so close, but she was here to have a good time so she wasn't going to make a thing out of it this once. When he turned her around, she spotted Carly over at the bar getting another tequila shot and Jules relaxed again, enjoying the rest of the dance.

Another song came on and it was a hard and fast tempo that she and Simone loved to jump around to, so she left the frat boy behind to find her friend. Simone was coming to find her as well. Colleen moved off to the side and took photos of them with her phone as usual, giggling.

When the song ended, the three headed back to the table and found Carly sitting there.

"What have you been up to?" Simone asked.

"Narrowly escaping the rough hands of the long haired man at the bar. I think I've had enough shooters for one night."

"We need food." Colleen picked up the small menu on the table and rattled off the appetizers. "Let's get the slider platter and the loaded cheesy bacon fries."

"Girl, just because you can eat like that and not gain an ounce doesn't mean we're all blessed with those genetics," Simone said.

Jules silently fumed. The girl didn't have an ounce of fat on her size six body. She didn't know what it meant to watch what she ate and yet she was always complaining about not being blessed with the right genes.

"Live a little." Jules snatched the menu from

Colleen. "I'll go order and be right back with a round of beer for us all. Longnecks or a pitcher?"

"Longnecks."

Jules took her time going to the bar to place the order. Her head was a little fuzzy from all the noise and dancing. But she felt good. Pumped, ready to face whatever tomorrow held with the final budget meeting.

The bartender set the four bottles on the bar and she grabbed them by their necks and headed back to her friends.

"Let's toast Carly and her new life," Jules announced, handing out the bottles. "Isn't that what we're here for?"

"Here. Here." Colleen raised her bottle.

Carly blushed and tried to hide her face behind her bottle, but Jules saw it. Boy, that Justin Porter had done a number on their friend that she still hadn't bounced back from.

The waitress came shortly after with the sliders and fries. The four talked, scarfed down the food, and then the girls showered Carly with the naughty gifts they'd brought.

Simone, as usual, gave something furry and leopard print in the form of handcuffs. Like Carly would actually tie a guy to her headboard and keep him her prisoner for the night. That was more Simone's style than Carly's.

"This one's from me," Colleen said, sitting down

another small, sparkly gift bag with bright tissue paper.

"Is there a theme to these gifts?" Carly asked.

"Yeah, that you use them," Simone said.

Jules joined her friends laughter as Carly reached inside the bag and pulled out a handful of glow in the dark condoms.

Wow. Who knew quiet little Colleen had it in her? Good for you, girl!

Carly's hand stayed suspended above the bag for a few seconds before she dropped the wrapped condoms back inside. She finally reached for the sedate white gift bag with pink tissue.

"Do I even want to look inside this one? It looks all innocent, but that means it's deceptive because it's coming from you, counselor."

Jules shrugged not about to give anything away. "Depends on how adventurous you are."

Carly slowly pulled out the pink tissue, and unwrapped the item. "Good heavens."

Jules smirked as Carly turned beet red inspecting the biker babe leather thong teddy and whip set that she'd purchased to draw out the hidden vixen in her friend.

Carly quickly wrapped the items back in the tissue and stuffed them into the gift bag again before cramming all the gifts into her large black bag.

"You guys didn't have to do this or bring these

here…tonight. You could have given them to me at my little apartment."

Colleen shook her head. "That place is so small. I swear, my linen closet is bigger."

Simone snorted, made a face, and then covered her nose and mouth with both hands.

"Sorry you don't approve, but it was all I could afford. I wasn't awarded alimony."

"Which is asinine!" Jules stood up. "That is the one thing about your divorce I don't agree with. How could the judge grant it without awarding you alimony? Justin Porter comes from money. Didn't one of his ancestors found that country club he belongs to?"

Carly nodded. "One of the first members. But his family doesn't like to brag."

Simone snorted again. "Is that why he mentioned it so often when you were first dating?"

"Did he?"

"Yes." Jules tossed a used napkin on the table. "He got the house. While you moved into a tiny apartment that you barely can afford without any support. You have no job. Your parents aren't speaking to you because you left him, it's—"

"I have a job interview next week now that everything is settled and I can focus on not going to court every day."

"The legal system is screwy. Where is justice in the world?" Jules continued to fume. She wanted to hit someone and she knew her anger wasn't all because of the unfairness of Carly's divorce settlement. It had a lot to do with the budget cuts that were leaving the youth at her center without programs they desperately needed.

Colleen patted her on the shoulder. "It'll be okay. The youth center will find money somewhere to support the programs for the kids. There have been budget cuts before and the center has survived."

Jules kicked the leg of a nearby chair. "Not like these cuts."

"I'm sorry, Jules, I hadn't realized it had gotten so bad this week," Simone said. "Someone should have let me know when I got back in town from my business trip."

Jules shook her head. "Enough about me. It's Carly's night out and we still have plenty of time before the bar closes. Another round of drinks? A round of pool?"

"A little pole dancing for our divorcee?" Simone suggested, getting to her feet and trying to persuade Carly to join her up on the stage. "You are not going to find Mr. Right Now if you stay hidden behind a table all night. You gotta get out on the dance floor and move your moneymaker."

"No. I've had too much to drink and my stomach isn't feeling up to it," Carly said.

"Okay, then what would you like to do?"

Colleen asked, reaching out and taking her hands in hers. "We're here to please."

"I want to spend time with my besties. Is that so wrong? I know you think I need to have a hot night out, but have I drawn a man to me tonight? Well, other than Mr. Longhair tattoo guy, but you know. Have either of you been propositioned? No. Is there something wrong with us?"

"I think we're sending off the wrong vibes," Colleen said. "We're woman, hear us roar, but stand your distance buster."

Jules smirked. "You got that right."

"More the reason we need to get up on the stage and shake our booties!" Simone left the table, went to the juke box and selected *Firefly* and went to the stage and proceeded to sway and gyrate.

Colleen ran to join her, laughing. They joined hands, raising their arms in a slow motion wave.

"What do you say, Carly?" Jules asked.

Carly shrugged. "What the hell. Let's get it on with Ed Sheeran."

As they joined their friends a few of the guys in the bar sauntered over and began dancing with them as well.

Jules was glad the frat boy from before hadn't approached her. If he had, she'd have felt he was getting way too familiar with her. Instead she ended up dancing with one of the executive types from downtown that liked to hang out at the bar.

She'd seen him around before, but he'd never been bold enough to approach her. She wondered what was different tonight.

They danced and shared small talk and before they left the dance floor he passed her his business card, which she stuck in her pants pocket. Parting ways, she went back to their table to finish her beer and catch her breath.

A bell rang near the bar and everyone stopped what they were doing. The bartender climbed up on the wooden surface and announced, "Last call of the night. We'll be closing in fifteen."

Wolf howls and cheering came from the group of frat boys and then a round of slaps on the backs of some of the guys.

"Wonder what that was all about?" Jules said looking at her friends who had gathered around her. They shrugged.

"Well, I hate to bail, but I have an early morning meeting." Jules slipped her arms into her blazer.

"On a Saturday?" Simone questioned.

Jules nodded. "With all the budget cuts we have to figure out how we're going to keep the few programs we still have from tanking."

"See you. Call if you need to talk." Colleen made a sad face before hugging her. When she pulled away, she looked at Carly and Simone. "I need to hit the ladies before we leave."

"Okay. We'll wait for you at the bar," Carly told her.

"Later, ladies," Jules headed for the door. She didn't really want to be going home early, but she had an obligation to her kids at the center to be there for them tomorrow at her best. And the only way she could ensure that she showed up that way was to get sleep tonight.

THE HEAT of the day had turned into a sultry Chicago night and she took her time walking, enjoying the sound of the waterfront in the distance. A sleek black car with tinted windows sped by her on the way to the 'L'. There was something off about the car that stuck out to her, but she couldn't quite put her finger on it, so she pushed the feeling away and focused on where she was going and her surroundings. She was a single woman walking at night. She couldn't afford to let her guard down. However, the further she walked the more the feeling nagged at her.

She'd gotten about a block away from the bar when she heard what she thought sounded like a gunshot. She stopped in her tracks and listened closely, but she couldn't be certain she'd heard correctly. But in an instant, the black car that had sped by came back to mind more clearly and she had a flash of memory of a sticker on the car that she'd seen around the youth center. The sticker was of two intertwined snakes. Twin cobras. A local gang in the area.

That's why the feeling wouldn't go away about the car. She reached into her blazer pocket for her cellphone, yet it wasn't there. She recalled placing it in the charging cradle at her apartment after talking to Carly. Damn. She hadn't picked it up before she walked out to catch the 'L'. She quickly scanned the area hoping by chance there was a police box nearby for emergency use. However, she didn't see one.

Time was ticking. She could either call for help or do something.

She turned around and began running back toward the Pied Piper as fast as she could. As she ran, all she could think about was she'd left Carly, Simone and Colleen there and a car with the Twin Cobras logo had been headed in that direction. She'd heard a gunshot. She was certain. It could have been a car backfiring. But what if it wasn't?

CHAPTER 2

WILL "LOVERBOY" McLeod packed his tactical bag alongside his three teammates after their last presentation for the Chicago PD promoting what the Brotherhood Protectors Security Team could do to aid law enforcement. A team like theirs could provide specialized protection to witnesses, aid in undercover investigations, or help keep citizens safe to free up local law enforcement to do their day to day jobs. It was just another way his boss Hank Patterson was trying to branch out and give his wounded warriors an avenue back into society. As a former Army Ranger, Will had the battle scars and the skill set to help with any problem put before him.

"That's the last of it." Wyatt Kincaid handed Liam Donovan a secured cable.

"Excellent." Liam stuffed the cable inside his bag before zipping it.

"I'll double check the podium area to make sure we didn't forget anything up there." Will took a step in that direction before Wyatt grabbed his arm.

"I already looked. We're good."

Their team leader Brand Chambers crossed the room and rejoined them.

"So are we ready to head to the airport?" Liam slung his bag on his shoulder.

"No. Hawkeye wants us to stay a while longer."

Wyatt checked his watch. "We're already cutting it close on catching our flight. Don Juan and Loverboy here might be able to sweet talk the attendant at the gate into letting us onto the flight, but they can't get us through security check points with our tactical gear any quicker than necessary."

Will punched him in the arm. "I'll have you know our skills come in handy as much as your ability to deal with PTSD victims, so don't knock it."

"Let's not squabble, guys," Brand ordered. "We'll still make our flight, even if we have to get a police escort to the airport or something. Let's double check to make sure we have all of our gear secured."

The three of them grumbled, but did the check anyway knowing how Brand was a stickler about securing their equipment. He'd been overly cautious ever since what happened to him in Afghanistan when his teammate hadn't packed their bag properly before they'd gone into theater. That teammate had died and the incident had left Brand injured with shrapnel in his chest too close to his pulmonary artery so he couldn't return to active duty.

While they rechecked everything, Brand wandered off to talk to Hawkeye again. Will looked up at his counterpart, Liam, and shook his head, but it appeared his teammate was off in la-la land.

"Hey, Don Juan," Will waved his hand in front of Liam's face. "Where'd you go there for a minute?"

Liam blinked, shaking the fog from his eyes. "What? Sorry. Did you say something?"

Wyatt laughed. "Yeah, man. We were asking if you were hungry. We were thinking if we time it right, we might have time to stop and get some grub on the way to the airport."

"You know me. I can eat anytime of the day and still want more." Liam patted his lean stomach.

Will pretended to hit him in the stomach. "One of these days, that lean muscle will go to pudge and you won't be able to eat like that. Then what will you do?"

Liam blocked his move and made a face, ignoring his question. "Hey, listen up. Here comes

Brand and Hawkeye. That look on Brand's face tells me we aren't leaving here tonight."

"What?" Wyatt turned, frowning. "I think you're right, Don."

Will didn't like the look on Brand's face either, but if they weren't leaving he knew it would be for a very good reason. He tried to relax, but it reminded him of the last twenty-four hours before he was due to return to the states from Iraq. There had been a typical delay in departure which ended with his regiment getting targeted before takeoff. The opposition had swarmed in on their base unit in the wee hours of the morning, leaving chaos in their wake. Their guard had been down because they were shipping out. Looking back now, it had been a stupid move on their part and several of his regiment paid for it. Three men had died and another six were injured. Leaving Chicago to go back to Montana would be nothing like that day, but he did feel an uneasiness wash over him like there was more in store than a simple delay.

TWO BLACK SUV police cruisers charged through the almost deserted Chicago streets toward the waterfront with lights and sirens blasting. The fact that their team was being thrown into an active case for Chicago PD immediately was a triumph for them and the success of their week long presentation. Will tried to sit still as the adrenaline pumped through his veins. He always got this way when his regiment was heading into theater. It didn't help that he'd overheard part of Hawkeye's phone conversation with Hank before they'd headed to the cruisers, laying out a rough sketch of Hawkeye's plan for the team and why they were not returning to Montana tonight. It had all sounded very favorable. It also sounded like Hawkeye had more than one assignment in mind for their team.

The cruisers arrived on the scene within minutes and Hawkeye led the way from the vehicles, stopping a few feet from where a woman argued with a detective who refused her entry into the bar.

"You don't understand! I was in there earlier with my friends. If I hadn't had to leave to catch the 'L,' I would have been with them when the shooting happened. I know they're still in there. I need to check to make sure they're okay."

Hawkeye turned to Brand. "That's Jules Gentry. One of your men needs to stay with her. As I understand it, she spotted the getaway car. I'll explain to the detective that your man is taking over."

Brand nodded.

"McLeod. She's yours. Find out what you can

about what she knows and make sure no reporters get near her."

"You got it."

Will followed Hawkeye over to the woman and waited while Hawkeye spoke to the detective before he approached her.

"So you were in the bar earlier tonight?" Will asked.

She pivoted and arched a brow. "That's right."

"But you left before the shooting."

"Correct."

Her answers were short and clipped, her stance going rigid and he knew she wasn't going to give him any more details without an introduction.

"I'm Will McLeod." He offered her his hand. "I've been assigned to protect you."

The woman looked surprised and she laughed, but stopped abruptly when she saw he didn't break a smile. "I thought you were joking. Why do you think I need protecting?"

"Because I say you do." Hawkeye stepped over and flashed his badge. "I'm Commander Burns with Chicago PD. McLeod here is going to be on you twenty-four/seven until I say otherwise. From what you told my officers and detective, you saw the shooters car and got the license plate number. You also can identify the specific make, model and markings on the car. You will make an excellent witness if this should go to trial. Those reasons alone are why you need protecting. The fact that this was a gang shooting is another. Do I make myself very clear, Ms. Gentry?"

The woman had opened her mouth halfway through Hawkeye's speech to protest, but she closed it and nodded her head in understanding.

"Very good." Hawkeye smiled briefly. "McLeod, take one of the SUVs and get her out of here before the media shows up. I'm surprised they haven't already attacked. My driver will drop you off wherever she tells you to go."

"What about my friends?" she asked as Will ushered her to the black SUV. "I have friends inside the bar. I want to know that they are safe."

"I have teammates here working to protect other eye witnesses. I can reach out and see if I can get information on your friends. Give me names, detailed description of what they look like and I will see what I can find out for you. That is the best I can offer at the moment." He opened the door to the back of the SUV and helped her climb inside before getting into the vehicle as well.

"That is more than anyone else has offered me. Thank you. I'm Jules Gentry. You can call me Jules."

"You can call me Will."

Jules' apartment was a nice place. She at least had a guest room with more than a futon sleeper. Which is what Will was used to crashing on when he visited his sister Cassie at Christmas. It was a full bed, not a twin, and he had his own bathroom.

"I had a roommate once. She left her furniture when she moved out so you got lucky or the room would have been bare."

"Cool." He dropped his tactical bag and duffle at the foot of the bed.

"The bed should have clean sheets on it. The bathroom hasn't been used in a while so if it isn't spotless that's why. But I can give it a cleaning tomorrow."

"I'll do it. Just show me to your supplies. I'll pull my weight around here."

She nodded. "Fair enough, Will McLeod."

"Just Will or McLeod, whichever you prefer. I answer to both. My friends also call me Loverboy because they say I'm a big flirt."

Her brow arched. "Is that right? Am I being forewarned?"

He shrugged. "I'm here to do a job, ma'am, and that's to keep you alive until you can testify against the gang that robbed the Pied Piper and killed that bartender."

Her mouth dropped open and her eyes grew round as saucers. She slowly shook her head back and forth. "Wh-hat? The bartender is dead?"

Oh crap. He'd just assumed with her outside of

the bar that she'd heard the scuttle butt between the officers on scene.

"I'm sorry. I shouldn't have blurted it out like that. I thought one of the officers or detectives would have mentioned the fatality."

"No. No one did." She ran a hand up her neck into her hairline and back down. "If they did I was too distracted trying to get them to let me into the bar to see my friends."

"Understandable, ma'am."

"Don't call me ma'am. I know that's a military thing, but Jules will be fine."

"I'll try to remember that."

"You're welcome to anything in the kitchen. If you don't need anything I'll see you in the morning. I have to be at a meeting at eight so I'll need to leave here by seven-thirty."

"Actually, I do need to talk to you about the events of the evening. If you'd rather wait until tomorrow to go over them because of your early appointment, I understand. But talking now, while everything is fresh would be best."

She pressed her lips together and looked at the floor. "Okay. Let's go back to the kitchen so we can sit at the table."

Will grabbed his notepad out of his tactical bag and followed her. Her short cut brown hair and the tailored blazer she wore gave off a no-nonsense air about her. He was interested to find out if that was true.

"Would you like something to drink while we talk?" she asked.

"I'm fine, but you go ahead if you need it."

She settled at the two-chair table, folded her hands in front of her and waited for him to speak.

"Let's start from the beginning. I know you were out with your three friends at the bar. You left them and were walking to the 'L,' then what?"

"I saw a black car speed by. At first I didn't realize it was a gang car. I just knew there was something off about it, something that stuck out in my mind that made me feel uneasy. But the further I went, the more I thought about that car. And then my brain focused in on the Twin Cobra sticker and I knew it was a gang car. I'd heard what sounded like a gunshot by then. I reached into my blazer pocket for my cellphone, but realized I didn't have it with me. Of course there wasn't a police box around for emergency calls. So I did the only thing I could think of, I ran as fast as I could back to the bar."

"And exactly how far had you gotten away, do you estimate, from the bar when all of this took place?"

"It was like a block, slightly less."

"But you were trying to get into the bar when we arrived."

"No. It only looked like that. I had been there talking to police officers and detectives. When I reached the bar, I immediately searched for the black car. I didn't go inside. I wanted to make sure I hadn't imagined the car had that sticker on it. I found where they had parked. I even got the license plate numbers and wrote them on a scrap of paper I found on the ground."

Will nodded. "Do you still have that?"

"No. The first detective I spoke to took it from me. And thanked me for my quick thinking."

"That was smart."

"I was headed back toward the bar when two of the guys came running out of there at top speed. I stepped into a doorway of another storefront so they wouldn't see me and watched them get in the car and drive off."

"Were you close enough to them to overhear anything they said to one another?" he asked.

She closed her eyes, her brow creasing. "The first guy said, just go! Then the other one said, get in the car fast. The first guy questioned him, are you sure? We can't leave him behind. The other one answered, are you kidding? He's dead. We'll be too if we don't get." She shook her head back and forth, finally opening her eyes and looking at him. "It makes me want to cry that I couldn't stop any of this."

"Don't feel bad. No one could have stopped

them." Will wrote everything she said down then looked up at her. "They believe the third guy is dead. The one they left in the bar. The one that we now know shot the bartender."

Jules slowly nodded.

"What happened next?"

"I finally made it to the bar, but by then the first police cars were pulling up and they wouldn't let me in. I started giving my statement and telling them what I knew. Then the detective arrived on the scene and I had to talk to him. That's when you guys showed up while I was trying to persuade him to finally let me go into the bar."

"So would you estimate that half an hour or more had passed by that point?"

"I'd believe that would be right."

Will nodded. "Is there anything else about tonight that you haven't told me or the police officers? Anything that you didn't remember at first, but maybe going over the events again has revealed to you?"

Jules bit at her bottom lip and then shook her head. "No. I think that's everything.

"What about a description of both of the guys that got away? Can you jot down what they both looked like for me?"

"Sure."

He slid his note pad over to her and she scribbled out a few lines before pushing it back across the table to him.

Will glanced at the pad. "I think that should do it."

"Good, because I really need to head to bed. I'll see you in the morning." She stood up and pushed her chair in.

"I'll be ready." He followed her down the hallway, stopping at the door to his room.

"Good night," she called.

Will went inside and stowed his tactical bag in the closet, then he sat his duffle in there as well. He plugged his phone in to charge and prepared to go to bed, smelling lavender as he turned down the sheets. He sat down on the mattress and removed his shoes, laid back testing the firmness and decided it was the right feel for sleeping. He hated a hard bed. He'd just as soon as sleep on the floor.

He closed his eyes and the next thing he knew, Jules was shaking him awake and calling his name. He grabbed her arms, sitting straight up in bed. "What's wrong?"

"Nothing. If you're going to shower before we leave you need to get up."

"Oh. Sorry." He released her.

"Did you sleep in your clothes?"

"Apparently I fell asleep when I was testing the mattress."

"I see the bed met your test." She smirked. "I'll

have eggs, bacon and toast ready for you when you get out of the shower."

"And coffee?"

"Of course."

"Thanks."

"No problem."

He hurried into the bathroom and rushed through his morning routine, not wanting to make her late for work. He decided to forgo shaving until after he ate, if there was time.

There wasn't. Jules was ready to walk out the door as soon as she wolfed down the food and drank her coffee. She needed to catch the seven-thirty-five 'L' to be at the youth center by ten till eight. Otherwise, she'd have to wait until the seven-forty-five 'L' and she wouldn't be there until eight, when the meeting started.

Will had just enough time to grab his phone and tactical bag before heading out with her. The ride to the youth center was quiet. Jules read over some report papers and Will sat watching the people get on and off the train car. He'd found the traffic for a Saturday morning heavy, but then Chicago was a busy city and people did use the 'L' as their mode of transportation to and from work. Not everyone had comfortable white-collar jobs, as was clear by the uniforms and name badges he saw hanging around peoples necks.

"Next stop is us," Jules said, slipping her papers

into the satchel she slung across her body. "The center looks a little rough on the outside, but don't let it fool you. We can't do anything about the exterior because of the neighborhood where it's located, but the interior is different."

She stood as the train slowed and he joined her, stepping toward the doors just before they slid open. They took the steps down two at a time and crossed the small plaza to a tree-lined walkway before they entered an older brick building that didn't look too shabby to Will. It wasn't anything as dilapidated as he'd expected after what she'd warned him about.

"I can't take you into the meeting with me. Is that going to be a problem?" Jules asked.

"No. I don't think one of your colleagues is a threat. Unless you feel for some reason someone that works here has in the past shown signs that they have gang affiliations?"

Jules giggled then stopped herself. "Sorry. I don't know why that should be funny, but if you knew us, you'd understand. We're all very boring individuals. I know this is a very serious situation, but I've been under so much stress this week. We're going through budget cuts which is why the administrators are here having a meeting on a Saturday morning." She led him down a long corridor, stopping at a closed door. Fishing in her satchel, she pulled out a set of keys and unlocked the door. "You can hang out in my office if you like or feel free to have a look around the center while I'm in the meeting."

"Okay."

"The recreation room will be buzzing with youth in an hour or so. And there might be a game of pick-up basketball out back on the court or in the gymnasium. Most of these kids crave adult attention so any you can give will be appreciated. And those who don't want it, well you'll be able to tell right away and know to back away."

"Got it."

She opened a desk drawer and pulled out what looked like a folded pamphlet. "This has a map of the facility so you won't get lost. There's vending machines down this corridor if you get hungry or need a soft drink. Coffee you can make in my Keurig. Mugs are clean. Drawer underneath the maker holds the coffee pods." She opened up another desk drawer and pulled out a single key on a stretchy band. "Here is an extra key to my office. Be sure to lock up if you leave here. Even to go to the men's, which is to the left four doors down."

"Got it."

She looked at her watch and took a deep breath. "Now, I gotta go or I'll be late for my meeting."

"Go. I'll be fine," he said.

.   .   .

THE DOOR HADN'T CLOSED until Will's phone buzzed and he looked to see who was trying to reach him. It was Brand wanting an update. He didn't have much to share, but he texted what he could, like Jules's description of the two gang members that had fled the crime scene.

"With Jules at Youth Center."

"Youth Center?"

"Where she works. Had a meeting today. Lots of teens here."

"Anything of interest to report?"

"Not yet. Keeping eyes and ears open. Out."

CHAPTER 3

WILL MADE himself a cup of coffee, took the map and key to the office, and locked the door before walking around the facility to get a better grasp of where things were located before it got crowded later in the day. He liked to familiarize himself with his surroundings. By the time he'd walked down several corridors he started hearing voices ... young, male voices, as well as the echoing thump, thump, thump of a basketball. He knew immediately he'd found the gymnasium.

He finished the cup of coffee before he opened the set of double doors and went inside. The five teens didn't acknowledge his presence at first. They kept right on playing. It wasn't until the ball got away from one of them and Will had to think fast to juggle the empty mug and catch the ball before making a rebound shot from where he stood.

The whoosh of the ball going in the basket had their dark eyes turning to look at him.

"Hey man! How'd you do that?" One of them called out.

"I couldn't make that shot with two hands."

The tallest of the bunch ran to get the ball. "You did it with one hand! Can you show me how do to that?"

"Who are you, anyway?" The next tallest asked.

"A friend of Jules."

"Oh, really?" The shortest said. "She's never brought a guy by here before."

Standing at five foot-ten, he wore a heavy gold chain around his neck, a red and black, rolled bandana tied around his head that matched Jules' description of what one of the gang members' wore around his head. The kid's white high tops looked fresh out of the box. There was no way he could afford those even if he had a part-time job making minimum wage.

One of the guys whistled, motioned with his finger and a girl came running from the direction of the bleachers. She took the empty mug from Will and ran back.

The guy with the ball passed it to Will and he dribbled it a few times, getting the feel of it as he eyed the basket from where he stood. It had been a fluke that the ball had gone in so easy the first time. He was out of practice, having left his basketball days in high school. When he was ready, he raised the ball up with his right hand and made the shot, hitting the basket again.

"Man, you have got to teach me that shot."

"It comes with lots of practice," Will said. "Shooting, missing, focusing, playing high school basketball."

"And you can still shoot like that?"

"It's like riding a bike. Once you learn, it's ingrained in your head," he explained. "I know you can learn to do it too with a little work. Squaring your shoulders with your foot position, focusing on the basket before you ever shoot."

"Ms. Jules is going to be in that meeting for a long time, so you got plenty of time on your hands to help us get it worked out," the kid with the high tops said.

"Yeah," the others chimed in.

"Sure. Why not." Will grinned. "First, I want each of you to show me what you got. No fancy moves, just honest shooting talent is all I care about seeing so I know where to start working with you on the technique. Let's see if I can remember what my coach taught me."

Each of the boys took turns making shots at the different distances that he asked, foul line, half court, and far right like he had been shooting. He made suggestions after each shot as to how the boys could improve, allowing them to make one or two shots with the new technique before moving on to the next position.

Will was surprised that they listened without ribbing each other or joking about it, but he could tell they were serious about the sport and wanted to improve their game.

They ended up doing a little three on three pickup game, but that didn't last long because the double doors to the gym slammed closed, distracting them. The basketball bounced to the sideline.

"Hey, Ms. Jules." The girls from the bleachers called.

"Girls."

"I believe this belongs to you," one of them said, handing her the coffee mug.

"Thanks." She looked in his direction. "I'm all finished for the day. Are you ready to go?"

"Sure. Unless you guys still need me to show you a few more pointers?" he said.

"No, man. I think we're all good here," the tallest one said. "Thanks for taking the time show us your moves."

"Anytime. Maybe I'll see you around next week," Will said. He ran over to retrieve the ball from the sideline.

"Yeah, right, like you'll be back," the kid with the high tops said.

"I will and you'll eat those words." He tossed the

ball to the kid before leaving the gym with Jules. "Sorry I lost track of time. I was exploring the facility when I ended up in here."

"No problem. At least you weren't bored in my office all morning." She smiled as they walked down the corridor back toward her office. "Is there anything in particular you'd like to do or need to take care of this afternoon?"

He chuckled. "Actually, that is what I was going to ask you, since I'm the one invading your space."

"I beat you to it. My Saturday is pretty open. I knew I was going to be working this morning so I've been taking care of errands in the evenings on my way home so I didn't have to do them all this afternoon. Can I show you around the city?"

"That would be nice. I've been here all week, but we didn't get to see much more than the inside of the CPD where we were holding the conference," he explained.

"Good." They stepped into her office and she closed the door behind them. "So if I do that for you, then maybe you can do something for me?"

"Within reason. I won't do or agree to anything that would put your life in danger."

"I'm not asking you to. I only want to know that my three friends are safe. Can I at least make a phone call to them? If not all three, one will do?"

He thought for a moment and decided that

wasn't anything that would put her in harm's way. "I think that can be arranged."

"Good. Let me put this mug in the kitchen dishwasher and I'll be ready to get out of here. Think about where in the city you'd like to explore while I'm gone."

JULES WAS STILL INWARDLY SMILING as they got off the 'L' at the Chicago Riverwalk District to explore the city. She'd used the same tactic with her protector as she did with the teens to manipulate the situation to get what she wanted. Normally it was just to get the teens to do what needed to be achieved like a structured activity, but with Mr. Will McLeod, she'd used this bargaining method to get a phone call to one of her friends. She could tell by his reaction she'd caught him off guard and she wouldn't be able to use the tactic again so easily. But that was okay. She didn't like using it unless she had to. And with her teens it was called for more times than she liked.

They explored the river walk area and she explained to him how it had taken many years of careful design and construction for the river to go from being a sewage dump to the beautiful landscape where the citizens of Chicago loved to hang out with family and friends. The architecture before them had been a master plan of the city that happened in several phases that had finally paid off with shops and restaurants, as well as water attractions from boat cruises, and ghost tours to keep the people coming back.

As they walked, they ended up at a street fair a few blocks away where they spent most of the afternoon combing through the vendors and exhibits. Jules found a scarf she liked and Will picked up a few t-shirts in black, navy, and gray. They even spent time sampling the many food trucks lined up along one of the streets. It was at that point that Jules thought she spotted Simone once, but when she stepped to get a closer look, the girl was gone.

"What is it?" Will asked. "Is your tamale no good?"

"No. I just thought I saw one of my friends in the crowd. Crazy right?"

"Maybe not. My buddy Don Juan might have ventured out to a place like this if he knew it was around. He loves to eat. But not knowing who he is assigned, I couldn't tell you for sure. I was assigned to you and the rest went into the bar, remember?"

Jules nodded.

"Do you know which friend you want to reach out to later when you make the phone call?"

"Yeah. Colleen. Carly would think I was checking up on her, and Simone, well, as much as I like the girl, she got on my nerves last night. She was trying too hard to draw attention to herself and push Carly in the wrong direction. So I think I will take a few days and let those feelings settle or I might say something I'd regret. Don't get me wrong, I want to know everything is alright with her, but…"

He nodded. "I have friends like that too. I know exactly what you mean. They can really push your buttons sometimes. I can check up on her if you like and report back without you having to get in touch directly. Not a problem at all."

"Thanks."

"Don't mention it. Now for something to drink. These chilies are a little hot. I need some more water or something a little stronger. What do you say?"

"These are great. You want to grab a few more tamales and take them back to my apartment? I can whip us up some margaritas there?"

His brow arched. "That sounds like a plan."

They went back to the food truck and placed their order to go, along with two bottles of water, before heading to the closest 'L' station.

While they waited on the train, Jules looked at Will. "I was glad to see you playing basketball with the boys earlier today. That was nice of you."

"Nice had nothing to do with it. I was enjoying myself. Plus I got to show off some moves I had forgotten about from when I played ball."

"Still, it was nice. They don't get many people to come into the center like that and give of their time freely."

The train arrived and they boarded, taking seats along the side together.

"I noticed one of the boy's wore a red bandana, a heavy chain, and some smart looking new kicks, while his friends didn't. Those are the same markers as the gang members who hit the bar, except for the Twin Cobra tattoos."

Of course you'd notice.

"You'll see boys and girls from all walks of life at the center. Those five were just a sampling of the kids that hang together."

Will turned toward her. "Don't get me wrong. I'm not trying to put them down. I'm just concerned about that kid. About whether he's running with the wrong crowd. Is he the prime age to be recruited by one of the gangs in town?"

She pressed her lips together and stared at him for a moment before finally speaking. "Yes, he is. And I worry about those boys every day. The other counselors and I try to give them other options besides gang life to choose from. We teach them decision making skills in the group activities we provide and we pray for the best when they are out on their own. We show them there are success stories by bringing in former center kids who have made something of themselves. But still the gangs win. The drugs win. Nine times out of ten they always win."

"We're gonna change that narrative."

He sounded so sure of himself when he said that. She almost wanted to believe he could...they could... but it was a pipe dream. She knew it because she'd had the same determination when she'd started at the center. Yet, she still had hope.

"How?"

"You let me worry about that for now. We've got the next several days together to figure it out."

She sat back against the seat and stared at him believing he would find a way. She also noticed he had a nice profile for someone so buff and muscular and who hadn't had a chance to shave that morning, but she didn't mind the gruff look on him. It was nice. It softened his otherwise domineering appearance, which she'd tried to ignore all day, but sitting this close to him and listening to him talk about coming into her youth center and making a difference just made him that more attractive to her.

Attractive.

Whoa, Jules!

Slow down girl. He's here to protect you. Not date you.

It had been a very long time since she had been attracted to anyone, but there was something very appealing about Will McLeod. And watching him with her boys from the center today had warmed her heart.

Maybe with his words and his physical appearance the boys would listen to him. Those five he'd been shooting hoops with earlier had taken to him quickly enough -- except for Rodrigo and his lip about how they wouldn't ever see him again -- but Will had promised him he'd be back. And she'd be glad to see the look on Rodrigo's face when he saw Will again.

"Our stop is next." She stood, grabbing the chrome pole for support as the train began to slow.

Will grabbed the pole a foot above her head and the braking of the train caused him to bump into her.

She looked up at him and smiled. "You'll get the hang of traveling the 'L' by the weeks end."

"Probably right when I'm ready to head back to Montana."

"Is that where you're from?"

"Not originally, but that's where my unit is based, in Eagle Rock, Montana."

"Chicago's a far cry from there."

"You can say that again."

She laughed and stepped off the train as soon as the doors slid open so he could follow her and they could get back to her place before their food got any colder.

. . .

BACK AT HER APARTMENT, Jules mixed the margaritas, blended them with crushed ice and put the tamales on to warm while Will checked in with his leader. She grabbed her phone and made her call as well. She decided to reach out to Colleen, but the call went unanswered. It didn't even go to voicemail, which was odd because her friend was meticulous about keeping her phone charged. She was a pharmaceutical representative so it was part of her job to be reachable. That put Jules on edge that something was up. She started to call Carly instead, but Will came back from his room, so she put down her phone. He'd said she could call one of her friends and she'd made that one call, even if she hadn't spoken to Colleen. She just have to try her again later. Maybe she'd have better luck then.

"Did you make your call?" he asked.

"She didn't answer."

"Same with my leader. I guess we'll have to try again later. Those tamales smell heavenly. I can't wait to eat more."

Jules smiled. "Grab a plate and help yourself while I pour the drinks. I'm more of a single-malt scotch drinker, but I do like a good margarita with my Mexican food."

"Single-malt scotch?" Will stepped back and eyed her for a moment. "Damn woman, I never would have pegged you for a scotch drinker."

"I blame it on my grandfather. He turned me

45

onto it at an early age. He liked his scotch and a cigar in the evenings."

"Do you smoke those as well?" Will asked.

She shook her head. "No. I draw the line at an old stogie. But I'd crawl up in his lap and he'd read the newspaper while he smoked and sipped his drink. And if I was good, he'd let me take a sip now and again. By the time I was a teen I was having a dram with him at night. My mom pitched a fit when she caught us, but the damage was already done. I had developed the taste for single-malt and when Gramps passed and we held his wake, I toasted him along with his friends."

"Drinking like that made scotch like mother's milk to you." Will shook his head, cutting into his tamales.

"Almost, but try telling that to my mother. It was a sore spot with her and gramps for the longest."

"Was he her father or your dad's?"

"Hers. If he'd been my dad's the man would've been out on the street quicker than you could have said Jack Frost. My mom didn't particularly care for my dad's side of the family and they didn't care for her either. That's the reason my parents didn't stay married but a few years. It's one thing when the husband and wife are having problems, but you add in the in-laws meddling and that makes for a bitter situation. It didn't end after the divorce either. It lasted until my dad's death, which they ultimately blamed on my mother because he was working three jobs just so I could take ballet lessons."

Will whistled.

"I had no idea he had been doing it, mind you. I was twelve …what did I know about finances? I had wanted to take lessons when I was six because I saw other little girls in their pink tutus and daddy signed me up." She shrugged. "It turned out I was good too, and I eventually was recommended to a different ballet school which cost three times that of the first one. Instead of doing the sensible thing, my father worked full-time, plus a part-time job in the evenings and another part-time job on the weekends. All because he had visions of me being a prima ballerina one day, mom said. He'd promised her if it got to be too much for him he'd stop, but a heart attack made that decision for him. Then my road to stardom ended as soon as my paid tuition ran out, budding ballet star or not. Mom had her hands full with her job and taking care of gramps at that point. She couldn't take on extra hours to afford the tuition, even if she could have gotten me in at another dance studio."

"That's a shame you had to stop dance alto-gether and that your father sacrificed his health like that."

Jules nodded, pushing her chair back to go get

the pitcher of frozen margaritas out of the refriger- ator to refill their glasses. "I continued stretching and practicing stances in my room every day. Then the youth center in Brooklyn Heights eventually offered some ballet classes. Nothing like what I had been accustomed to, but free is free and I did those. That's when I met the youth counselor who changed my perspective on life. She inspired me to work with youth and become a counselor as well."

"What about ballet? Do you still have a passion for it?"

Jules slowly shook her head. "I know what my dad did was out of love for me. He was trying to give me something special by making it possible for me to take the lessons and he saw my potential, but I'd rather have him here with me now than losing him all those years ago. Instead, I've lost him, mom and gramps all before I even turned thirty. I lost my grandma when I was a toddler so I don't remember her much. And because of the way my dad's family treated my mom, I never was close with them."

"Jules, you don't know that you wouldn't have still lost him when you were twelve. If it was his time to go, it was his time to go no matter if he worked one job or three."

She looked at him and half smiled. "I know you're trying to show me it wasn't because of my ballet that he died, and I appreciate it. I never blamed myself, if that's what you're thinking. Even later on when I thought back on losing him after my mom passed too, it never crossed my mind."

"I'm glad to know that, because it wasn't."

She bit her bottom lip, closed her eyes for a moment and took a deep breath before revealing more about her past. "I was one of the lucky ones, you know. If it hadn't been for my youth counselor guiding me in the right direction when I was in high school I wouldn't have the college education I have today. She took an interest during my mom's illness. She made sure that I kept my grades up. She helped me apply for scholarships and grants to cover all costs. I never had to take out a loan. That is why it's so important that I try to keep programs at my youth center from being cut. I want the kids who come there to have every opportunity that I was given and more. I want to give back as much as I can to make a difference in their lives as was made in mine."

Will drummed his fingers on the table for a moment. "You are one person, Jules. Sometimes it takes a village to move a mountain."

"Or a wealthy donor." She sat back in her chair and smiled. "Someone stepped up and made a substantial anonymous donation last night. We learned about it in our meeting this morning."

"That's terrific news. Why didn't you tell me? We could have celebrated tonight."

She was surprised by the way his face lit up at

her news like he really cared about the youth center getting the funding it needed as much as she did.

"You don't think having margaritas and tamales in my kitchen is celebration enough?" she asked.

He tilted his head, reached for his glass and raised it. "I think it is a darn good one, Jules Gentry. Thank you for letting me be a part of it."

She raised her glass and they clinked them together before drinking. "Now tell me about you, Will McLeod. I've let my food get cold rambling on more than I should. It's your turn to tell me how you became part of this Brotherhood Protectors and how you ended up in Chicago to be assigned to me."

He grinned and sat down his glass. "My story is nothing compared to yours."

"I'll be the judge of that. Can I get you another tamale? I'm going to warm my plate real quick in the microwave."

"As good as they are, I think I've reached my limit for now. Maybe later."

WILL PUSHED BACK from the table and thought about her question. He didn't think she really wanted to hear about him joining the Brotherhood Protectors as much as what got him there, what *really* got him there: his home life that led him to joining the army. He wasn't sure he was ready to open up to her about that, but she'd freely told him about her past, which he'd found surprising. She hadn't come off as someone who'd divulge information about herself to a total stranger that easily. Counselors normally weren't the type.

"I grew up with a single parent. My dad raised me and my sister, Cassie. We lost our mom when we were young. Her job called for her to travel often and one trip the train she was on derailed…" he cleared his throat. "Dad did the best he could for us. We had our grandparents on both sides. He eventually remarried and Margaret was great. She tried her best to be there for us and we liked her, but she wasn't our mom. I guess it came across more than Cassie and I realized. Margaret left us after six years, saying she couldn't go on feeling like an outsider in the family.

Cassie and I blamed ourselves for not making more of an effort with her, but dad, he just zoned out. He didn't even try to protest when the divorce papers came. Eventually, Cassie went away to college, dad sold the house and moved to a small apartment near his work, and I moved in with my grandparents on my mom's side while I finished high school. That's when I decided to enlist in the army after graduation."

He looked at her for a moment to see if she showed signs of regretting asking him about his past, but she didn't. She genuinely looked interested. So he trudged forward.

Taking a deep breath, he let it out slowly. "I felt I lacked direction of what I wanted to do with my life, but I knew I had to get out of town. I didn't want to stay there and be a burden on my grandparents any longer. Not that they ever said I was one – what grandparent would – but I knew they didn't sign up to have a teen in their house for that long a period at their age. So I got out as soon as I could."

"Did you stay in touch with them after you enlisted?" Jules asked.

"Of course. After basic I went back before shipping out again. Cassie was home from college at that point and we had a little family reunion. I even saw my dad for the last time before he passed." Will finished his margarita and pushed further away from the table. He bent forward, resting his arms on his knees and stared at the floor. "My dad had truly lost his will to live after Margaret left. He did what he had to do to keep his job to survive, but eventually that wasn't enough. There were layoffs and that was the breaking point for him. He couldn't find work and retraining at his age ... at least that is what Cassie told me later when we talked."

There was an awkward silence in the room and

he searched for something to say as he picked at imaginary lint on his cargo pants.

"Were you able to come in for his funeral?"

Will shook his head, but didn't look up, afraid he'd choke up if he saw pity in her eyes. That was the one thing he couldn't take right now.

"I didn't find out about his death until two weeks after they'd buried him. Cassie tried to get word to me. She'd held off as long as she could before having the services, but I was stationed in a no communication zone at the time. Once word finally reached command and I was notified, I was given the option of leave, but after I talked to Cass, we agreed it was best for me to stay put and finish the last month of my tour before coming home."

Jules laid her hand over his and that startled him. There was warmth and when his eyes met her chocolate ones, he saw concern in them, not the pity he'd feared.

"You know." He took a jagged breath and shook his head. "I didn't make it home as planned. I was approached to join the Army Rangers at the end of my tour and was routed to special training immediately. When I called Cass, she told me to go for it, to shoot for the highest rank so I never had to look back with regret."

"And did you tell her to do the same thing?"

He jerked his head up and looked at Jules. "Yeah. How'd you guess?"

"I get the feeling you both support one another that way."

"We do."

Jules looked away, but not before he saw what looked like glistening in the corner of her eyes. Was that unshed tears?

He noticed she reached up and swiped at her eyes and cleared her throat before she spoke. "I'm going to clean up."

"Can I help?"

"There isn't much. It'll all go in the dishwasher and I'll run it for the week. Why don't you go give your sister a call?"

He grinned. "How'd you know I was thinking about doing that?"

She shrugged. "A counselor's intuition."

CHAPTER 4

JULES SLEPT in as she normally did on Sunday mornings. When she finally showered and ventured from her room, she found Will shirtless in a pair of shorts, doing pushups on her living room floor. Sweat glistened on his skin and his already ripped muscles bulged even more with each repetition.

Unable to take her eyes off him for several moments, she felt heat rise up her body and she forced herself to look away. She swallowed and tried to find her voice to speak. "You know, there is a gym downstairs that you can use. All tenants have access."

"Exactly, tenants." He didn't stop moving up and down as he spoke. "I don't have the code to get into the gym."

She noted he hadn't sounded winded. She bet his stamina in the bedroom was impeccable and he could go several rounds without needing rest. She silently groaned.

Get a grip, Jules!

"Oh…Right…I-I guess I need to give you that." She went to her satchel and found a notepad, jotted down the code and laid it on the floor in front of him.

"Thanks."

"No problem. Have you eaten? Would you like…"

"I've been up for hours." He got to his feet, picking up the paper with the code on it. "I'm going to go grab a shower and then we can head out for brunch if you want?"

"Brunch. Yeah. That sounds good." She waited until he was gone before she went to the refrigerator and grabbed a bottle of water, downing in it in several gulps.

It wasn't like her to react this way. What had gotten into her? She was acting like she imagined Simone would. Speaking of her friends, that reminder her that she had never tried Colleen back. She dialed her number and waited for it to ring. It did several times, more times than it should before Colleen's voice mail should have come on, the same as the day before. It really bothered Jules.

It wasn't like Colleen to go off the grid without telling anyone, unless there was nothing wrong at all and she was just having issues with her cell provider. That had happened before she switched to the private company through work since she is a pharmaceutical representative.

Jules ended the call and laid her phone on the kitchen counter, tapping her nails in repetition on the granite as she thought of trying another friend. Maybe Carly? But, the probability of Carly being home at this hour was unlikely. She typically went to church, but would she go today? With a body guard in tow? Bringing a strange man with her so soon after her divorce was finalized would bring up lots of questions. No, Carly wouldn't go.

She reached for her phone and dialed Carly's number, but before the call went through, Will came back into the room dressed from his shower. She quickly ended the call and slipped her phone in her jeans pocket.

"You ready to go?" She asked.

"You still not having any luck getting ahold of your friend Colleen?"

His question surprised her.

"How'd you guess?"

"I saw that same worried frown yesterday. If it makes you feel any better, I haven't had any luck checking in with my unit leader either. Not sure what is going on there. But I'm not going to worry. He'll reach out when he can. He always does."

"When he *can*?" Jules said, her voice escalating in volume. "That doesn't make me feel better. He's assigned to one of my friends. What if that means one of them is in danger?"

"Calm down, Jules. Don't jump to conclusions."

She shook her head. "I don't think going out for brunch is such a good idea after all."

"On the contrary, Ms. Gentry. We are going out. I'm getting you out of this apartment and getting your mind off of your friends with good food, good company, and hopefully good drink. You just have to point us in the right direction."

It took about five minutes to get her out of the apartment and another five to get down to the 'L'. Then they were on their way to the Riverwalk area where dining options were plentiful and they could find lots of attractions to keep them busy for the afternoon. Will noted that despite the sun shining bright in the sky, the wind was a bit breezy and brought with it a chill that wasn't there the day before. He understood why Jules had worn another blazer and suggested he grab a jacket.

Despite the change in temperature, the Riverwalk was just as crowded as well. People were out on the water in their boats, cruising up and down the waterfront, as well as catching the rays on the steps. Outdoor seating was filled at the eateries and it was easier to get a seat indoors than out, which was fine with them.

Jules requested a booth away from the windows and the hostess found them one that still gave them ample view of the waterfront.

"You need to relax. Just because I haven't heard from Brand doesn't mean that Carly, Simone, or Colleen are in danger. Neither does you not being able to reach Colleen either. She may have forgotten to charge her phone. It's as simple an explanation as that."

"I'd still feel better if I could just talk to one of my friends. Maybe I should try to call Carly instead...or even Simone."

"If that will ease your mind then do it, but keep the call short. Under three minutes if possible so a hacker can't trace your location."

"A hacker?"

"You have a smart phone. A hacker can infect your phone with malware from social media that will attach itself to your contacts and weave an infectious web around you and anyone you come in contact with on your phone. Think about it."

She made a face of disgust. "That makes me want to wear protective gloves every time I touch my phone again."

He grinned. "Sorry. Just answering your question."

"Then I suppose my suggesting you reach out to one of your other team members is out of the question?"

"It isn't." He picked up the menu in front of him. "I will. Later. After we return to your apartment. But right now, I'm starving and I'm ready to have some food."

Once they placed their food order, he got her talking about her grandfather again and she was soon relaxed, sipping her water and smiling. But all that changed when the cork of a champagne bottle popped at a nearby table. Jules jumped, knocking over her glass of water in the process and it would have spilled all over the white linen table cloth if he hadn't sprang out of his chair and leaned across the table to catch it.

"Sorry," she murmured. "I don't know why I reacted that way."

He cocked a brow at her. "Really? Do you care to rethink that statement?"

A slow smile hinted at the corners of her mouth. "I stand behind my declaration."

"It's a startle reflex. The cork popping sounded like gunfire and caused you to jump. There's no mystery there."

Jules opened her mouth to protest, but before she said anything their food arrived. Instead, she smiled at him and once the waiter was gone said. "You think you know everything?"

"I have a pretty good idea of the situation at hand."

She shook her head before cutting into her food, leaving him in silence to do the same.

Will missed the chit chat they'd shared the day before as they'd eaten the tamales at the food truck and then continued their meal at her apartment. He'd only been teasing her, but obviously he shouldn't have about the cork sounding like gunfire, especially not so soon after she'd heard gunfire outside of the Pied Piper bar.

Damn.

Not your best move, McLeod. He silently chided himself.

She was worried about not being able to get in touch with her friends and that was the whole point of bringing her out to eat, to get her mind off of it all.

Damn.

"I'm sorry."

Jules stared at him for a moment. "About what?"

"For being so insensitive about the cork popping to tease you about your reaction. Of course you'd jump so soon after hearing that gunfire on Friday night."

"It's okay, Will. I'm not upset. I'm embarrassed. I'm a counselor. I'm supposed to know how to handle situations like these for others and yet, I can't even do it for myself."

He shook his head. "I don't think anyone in your situation is supposed to be able to deal with it like that. I think even counselors need their own counseling at times to get past trauma. Not that you've been in that severe of a position. But you shouldn't feel like you have to be the one to self-analyze."

Will laid down his fork discovering the more he talked the less of an appetite he had. He noticed that she'd stopped eating as well, which was a shame because the food had been really good.

"Do you need a box to go?" he asked.

She looked down at her plate in surprise and nodded. "They really do serve large portions here."

"I was thinking the same." He spied their waiter and motioned for him to come over and asked for the boxes and the check. The waiter obliged, but not before he asked if they'd like to see the dessert menu, which they declined.

After paying their checks, they window shopped down the riverwalk for a while. Will carried their to-go boxes in the restaurant's paper tote, until Jules found a store she just had to go into.

"Do you mind?" she asked, giving him a sheepish look that reminded him of his sister. "I wouldn't go in, but they're having a big sale today and I've had my eye on a blazer for some time."

"Go on."

"They have a good selection of men's clothes in the back if you need anything while you're here."

"I could use a few more things other than my tactical gear. I didn't exactly come to Chicago for an extended stay."

"Exactly," she agreed a little too eagerly.

"Are you saying you don't like my clothes, Ms. Gentry?" He cocked a brow at her.

"No. No. Not at all. I-I was agreeing that shopping when there is a sale on wouldn't hurt anything. That is all I meant."

He grinned at her. "Sure you did."

She finally wagged a finger at him. "Oh you. You had me going there for a minute."

He chuckled as she opened the door and they went inside. She pointed him in the direction of the men's section and she headed to the ladies agreeing they'd meet back up whenever the other was finished.

Will was certain he'd finish before her. He wasn't one to spend much time debating about colors or styles when shopping, yet he was still deciding on a pair of casual slacks when Jules strolled back with her purchase already in a shopping bag.

"Having trouble deciding?"

"Whether to go with just jeans or if I should get something a little more dressy as well in the event I need it while here. The sale price is a real bargain."

"Go with the navy if you are getting the slacks to go with those pullovers," Jules said.

"Is it always that simple for you?" he asked.

"What?"

"Making difficult purchase decisions?"

She smirked, reached down and picked up the restaurant tote. "That wasn't a difficult decision. It was practical. Bargain buying is always practical. I'll wait for you up front."

He gathered his purchases up and went into the dressing room to try everything on before buying. He'd learned long ago because of his muscle mass that sizes were not all alike. Luckily everything fit and he was able to meet Jules up front within minutes once he made the purchase.

"Where to now?" he asked. He took the restaurant tote and sat it inside the larger store bag he carried with his purchase. He offered to put Jules plastic bag in his as well and she agreed.

"I suppose we could head back to the 'L' and my apartment," she said. "Unless you want to explore more of the city?"

He thought about that for a moment as they walked along the river walk, retracing their path from either and then asked, "What time do you normally report for work?"

"Eight, like yesterday," Jules replied.

"Why so early?"

"Why not? It gives me time to get prepared for the day before the rest of my team members arrive. I like the quiet, the solitude."

"Then you must hate having me in your personal space at home."

"I never said that. I did have a roommate before, remember."

He nodded. "Tell me about her. Was she a friend or a colleague?"

"Neither at first, though we had become companions by the time she'd moved out. We keep in touch. Christmas and birthday cards and such."

Jules smiled and the look that crossed her face made him think she was remembering a fond memory she'd shared with the woman. It was nice to know she'd had others beside her friends from the bar to lean on over the years.

"So shall we head to the 'L' then?" he asked to confirm that is where they were headed.

"Absolutely."

For a Sunday afternoon, the 'L' car was deserted and Will was glad. He liked it that they had the space to themselves as they rode to their destination. Jules prattled on about an event coming up that they'd seen a poster for in the station. She'd really wanted to go to it, but the main event had sold out before she got off work and could call about getting tickets.

"Why didn't you call during work?" he asked.

"I wish I had had the time. I was in meetings back to back all day. We didn't even get to stop for lunch. It was ordered in." She frowned. "If I had only thought to have gotten Colleen to call and get the tickets for us."

Will held his breath at the mention of her friend, but she didn't miss a beat wanting to know why they couldn't reach her or his leader. Instead she shook her head.

"Maybe a radio station will have tickets that they'll be giving away," he suggested.

"Maybe." She rose from her seat as the car began to slow and he followed suit to get off the train.

"I've enjoyed our day," Jules said as they took the stairs down from the 'L' platform to the street.

"I have too." Will observed their surroundings, the moderately light flow of pedestrian traffic, and almost no cars passing on the street. Most people in the neighborhood used the 'L' for transportation. A few cars were parked along the street as they were before they left to go into the city.

"I need to get coffee." Jules announcement caught him off guard and before he knew it she was gone, darting across the street, between two parked cars toward the little supermarket on the other side.

"Wait. You can't …" before he could even get the words out he saw the first parked car at the corner gun it.

"Jules!"

CHAPTER 5

WILL RAN with the shopping bag as fast as his feet could carry him toward Jules, reaching her seconds before he imagined the car would have clipped her backside. Instead, he grabbed her around the waist and pulled her back against him with his free arm. She screamed and he spun away from the car like he was a quarterback in possession of the football. He would have made it to the end zone for the goal or the sidewalk if he hadn't put them in the path of a kid on a skateboard.

He hadn't seen the teen in time and there was no way to pivot out of his path or make his feet move any faster. The skateboarder did try to veer around them but there wasn't much room with the parked cars. A collision was inevitable and Will braced himself and a squirming Jules the best he could.

"What do you think you're doing, McLeod?" she screamed seconds before the skateboarder plowed into them and they fell backwards into the street with a thud.

"Ugh," Will groaned.

Jules head slammed back against his mouth forcing his own head to connect with the pavement. He swore he saw stars for a moment as he tried to catch his breath.

"Man, watch where you're going," the teen grumbled.

"Watch where we're going?" Jules questioned, breaking free of Will's hold. "You plowed into us. There's a city ordinance about skateboarding on the street and sidewalks. You're only allowed in the skate parks."

"Call the police why don't you," the teen said, grabbing his board and scurrying away.

Jules got to her feet, feeling a little shaky from the jolt of the impact. She noticed Will hadn't made a move to get up yet and a crowd of by-standers were gathering around them.

She knelt back down and shook Will's shoulders, noticing he still clutched the shopping bag. "Hey, are you okay?"

"Yeah." She heard him say even though his eyes were still closed. "Give me a moment to catch my breath."

"Sure."

"Foolish woman, didn't your mother ever teach you to be more careful than to dart out into the street between parked cars?"

"Of course she did," Jules said, looking at the crowd that had gathered. She spotted a face she recognized from the youth center. Rodrigo, for a split second their eyes locked before he faded into the crowd. She found it odd that he'd be in her neighborhood on a Sunday because he didn't live anywhere near here.

She slowly rose and took a small step to see if she could spot him again.

"Then why'd you do it?"

"What?" She looked back at Will and he was sitting up.

"I asked why you would run between two parked cars out into the street."

"I saw there was no traffic coming. It was perfectly safe."

"It wasn't or you wouldn't have almost been hit by that car that I saved you from."

Jules frowned, stepping back toward him and offering a hand to help him up. "But you didn't save us from the skateboarder. Some bodyguard you are."

He only grunted getting to his feet. "I'll remember that the next time and just let you get hit."

"But I see you did save the leftovers and our shopping."

"Of course. Priorities."

"In all seriousness." Jules walked around him. "Are you hurt anywhere? Are you okay? I can't begin to thank you for saving my life. You're right. It was a stupid move even if the road was clear. That car came out of nowhere."

"Not nowhere. It was parked at the corner and gunned it when you stepped into in the cross walk."

"It did?" She halted in front of him and tried to hide her shock, but knew she did a poor job of it. "Why?"

"That's what I'm going to find out as soon as I can get ahold of footage of this area. There has to be a license plate captured from a store security camera."

A patrol car came by about that time and the by-standers slowly dispersed to different sides of the street. An officer got out of the car. "What's going on here…? McLeod is that you?"

"You're known by name?" Jules asked.

"Apparently so," he said before doing an about face. "TJ, good to see you. I didn't know you ran patrol."

"As a sergeant, I get in the field as much as I can to support my men, especially on Sundays. I thought you and your team were headed out of town after the session on Friday?"

"We were, but we got called in to assist with the Pied Piper."

"Good. Good. Hawkeye was smart to use you guys on it. So back to what's going on here. I got the call that a car almost hit a pedestrian."

"Yes," Jules said. "I was the intended victim, but Will saved me."

The officer looked at her for the first time and nodded. "Intended victim? You think it was intentional?"

"Yes."

"And do you know why the car tried to hit you?"

"No. I was in the cross walk. Nothing was coming and it pulled from where it was parked and gunned it toward me."

Will step toward TJ. "That's what I'd like to find out. I don't suppose you could help me get security footage of the area to see if we can get a license plate?"

TJ looked at him. "Is she an eye witness in the Pied Piper?"

Will nodded.

"So this might be connected?"

"I need to rule it out."

"Say no more. I'll get in touch with Hawkeye and see what we can get for you."

"Thanks. Hawkeye's got my information so he can get in touch with me when he does."

"All right then. I'll see if I can get a few witness statements and wrap things up."

"I'm going to run in and get the coffee," Jules said. "Or rather I'll walk in to get it," she amended when Will glared at her.

"I'll come with you." Will took a step in her direction to follow, but she stopped him.

"I'm fine, really. I won't be but a minute."

JULES KEPT an eye out for Rodrigo in the crowd as she made her way into the corner market, but she didn't see him. She still found it odd that he would be in this part of town so close to her apartment, so close to where she lived. That thought unnerved her. Did the kid even know this was where she lived? If so, how'd he find it out? Had he followed her from the youth center without her knowledge? She tried to always be aware of her surroundings, but if he had then it meant she had let her guard down and put herself in danger.

Prickly fingers crawled up and down her spine at those thoughts. She'd get to the bottom of this tomorrow. She tried to put the thoughts out of her mind because she couldn't do anything about it today. The best she could do is ask him about it the next time she saw him.

The thought that maybe it hadn't been him at all, but a kid that looked like him ran across her mind. Nah. She'd locked eyes with him long enough to know it was Rodrigo. He stared right back at her with that I-dare-you-to-blink-first manner of his. She'd had too many one on one conversations with him not to know that look.

She grabbed her favorite brand of coffee and on the way back to the front saw a package of muffins she thought would be good for breakfast tomorrow, so she got those too before proceeding to the register. If it were only her, she'd forgo trying to have breakfast every day and just grab a granola bar out of the vending machine at the youth center. However, she had a guest staying with her and she needed to think of Will and his needs too.

By the time she returned to the street the patrol car was gone and the crowd had totally dispersed. Will was waiting for her outside the market doors. He had a grim expression on his face as if he wasn't too pleased that she wouldn't let him go into the market with her.

"Ready?" he asked.

"Yeah."

"That doesn't sound convincing."

"I'm still a little shaky, I guess. The adrenaline rush is easing off. My brain is starting to process what happened more clearly now. I'm feeling the real danger I was in."

"Understandable."

"If it hadn't been for you, I would be dead."

"Maybe not. You might have had a broken hip and leg from being hit."

She glared at him. "Gee, that sounds so much better. Stuck in the hospital and rehabilitation for weeks."

"It beats being six feet under."

She thought about what he said as they walked and found herself limping, a pain in her leg and hip radiating at the mere thought of what he had said. She rubbed it. Catching what she was doing, she shook herself out of the psychosomatic moment, hoping he hadn't noticed her. She knew what was wrong with her. It was the whole idea that Rodrigo had been in the crowd. He had been there when she'd almost been hit. He was being groomed for a gang. She knew it. They'd talked about it and ways he could avoid going down that path if he wanted it. The operative word being "if" he wanted it. She'd really thought she'd been making inroads with him even if he still wore those white kicks and the gang bandana. But she couldn't help wonder if Rodrigo being here today wasn't part of some initiation task. What if he'd followed her and Will from down town? It was a possibility.

WILL WATCHED as Jules rubbed her hip and limped a few steps more. It had been the funniest thing he'd ever witnessed. He mentioned a broken hip and leg and then she went to limping. But he wasn't about to say anything about it either. He saw the worried (or was it just a deep in thought look?) that was on her face. There was definitely something on her mind that she wasn't ready to tell him about. He could live with that. She didn't have to confide in him as long as she didn't keep things from him that would put her in danger. That was where he'd draw the line. They continued on until they came to her apartment building and went up.

"Here's the leftovers," he said, "if you're going to the kitchen?"

"I am." She looked into the bag. "Thanks for keeping them so safe during the ordeal. The containers are in perfect condition."

He shrugged. "It's all in a day's work, ma'am."

She cackled, going to the kitchen. She put the coffee container in a cabinet, washed her hands and dried them before she finally opened up the refrigerator and set the food containers inside, but when she shut the door, she slid down it to the floor and began bawling.

He rushed to her, but she put a hand out to keep him at bay, shaking her head as she fought to regain control.

"S-so…s-sorry." She finally managed. She quickly wiped her face with her hands, removing any moisture from her eyes with her fingertips.

"I'm okay. Just pent up emotion that had to come out."

"I get it. And it's okay to show it. To let those feelings out."

She took a deep breath and exhaled slowly. Then she took another breath and let it out in short huffs. "I'm a counselor. It's hard for us to do that sometimes. We're used to dealing with others' feelings, not our own."

"I'm honored you felt comfortable enough to show your emotions in front of me."

Her head snapped up and her eyes enlarged as she stared at him. She pulled her bottom lip into her mouth with her top two front teeth, then released them, opening her mouth fully as if to say something, but stopped. Instead, she gave him a nod and got to her feet, refusing his hand.

"I'm going to go hang up my blazer," she said.

He watched her take her bag from the larger shopping bag and disappear into her room.

He'd obviously said the wrong thing.

JULES STAYED in her room with the door open as long as she could that afternoon to avoid facing Will while she figured out why it bothered her so much what he said. So what if she had felt comfortable enough with an almost total stranger and showed her emotions when she broke down and cried? But Will wasn't really a stranger. He was her protector. He was there to keep her safe. Hadn't he proved that already today when he kept that car from hitting her?

The more she thought of it, the more it irritated her. She didn't show her emotions to her friends that easily and here she was showing them to him. Why Will? Why now?

Albeit this wasn't the most natural situation in the world. Her friends had been in a bar where a shooting had occurred and she'd witnessed the shooters going to the bar and two of them coming out.

Her friends. She hadn't been able to get a hold of Colleen and when she tried Carly she'd had to end the call because Will had come back to the room. Maybe she should try again now that Will had given her the green light?

She reached for her cellphone, but the face of Rodrigo flashed before her eyes and she cringed. What if he'd been at the scene today watching her? What if he'd been following her for the gang and she'd been unaware of it for weeks? What if someone had tampered with her phone, infecting it was a malware virus that could lead the gang to her and her friends? The thought of being the reason that happened terrified her.

She busied herself reorganizing her already tidy closet trying to take Rodrigo, the accident, the bar shooting, her friends, and ultimately Will off her mind. When she finished that, she read the last few chapters of a book she'd been reading before she finally ventured back to the kitchen to investigate those leftovers from brunch.

"Will, I'm going to have something to eat. Are you hungry?" she called when she saw he wasn't in the living room. There was no answer so she walked down the hallway to his room and the door was open, but he wasn't inside.

That was odd. He'd left without telling her? Or had she not been paying attention to what was going on in the apartment that she hadn't heard him?

She immediately assumed he went down to the gym so she didn't think anything more about it as she heated up her leftovers.

She was almost finished when the door opened and he came in from his workout.

"Have a good time?" she asked.

"Yeah. That gym is great. Thanks for the code."

"I already ate my leftovers if you're hungry."

"Thanks, but I had a sandwich before I went to work out. I might order a pizza later if you're game."

She groaned without thinking. "You're going to be bad for me, McLeod."

He grinned. "Why do you say that?"

"You know how to talk to my stomach. All

we've done this weekend is eat rich food. If we continue like this I'm going to be headed for Weight Watchers."

He laughed, but she thought she heard him say "as if" as he sauntered down the hall and disappeared through the open door to his room. That made her smile.

She cleaned up her dish and made two lunches for tomorrow before going back to her room to pick out what she was going to wear to work the next morning. That was half the battle of getting ready in the mornings for her. Then she went back to the kitchen and prepared the coffee maker to turn on to brew for them. They had the muffins she'd picked up at the corner market for breakfast.

She had just settled in the living room and turned on the television when Will came back through talking on his cellphone.

"Thanks, Hawkeye. I'll be in touch."

She turned down the volume with the remote. "That sounded promising?"

He shrugged. "He was finally getting back to me about the incident earlier today."

"Oh."

"He's had a busy day. Nothing bad." Will shrugged again. "Anything good on the tube?"

"It's Sunday night."

"Say no more."

Her eyes followed him as he walked over to the

refrigerator and opened the door, taking out a bottle of water. He looked back at her and caught her watching him. But she didn't look away.

"Do you want one?"

"Sure."

He returned and joined her on the sofa. "I'll trade you for the remote."

They made the exchange and while she opened the bottle he channel surfed until he found a movie they both agreed upon. Instead of ordering pizza, she popped a bag of popcorn, dumped it into a large bowl and they enjoyed it over glasses of wine.

By the time they went their separate ways and turned out the lights, Jules was convinced that Will McLeod was more than a protector, he was a very versatile man. If they'd met under different circumstances, she could see herself taking a play out of Simone's book and going for it and she didn't find herself in that situation often.

CHAPTER 6

WILL SPENT most of the day checking out the youth center to make sure the place was locked down tight. Jules was able to get him access to more than the pamphlet map he'd used on Saturday. With the help of the day janitor, he had access to parts of the facility that only those looking to do harm would venture. But as it turned out, no one had yet and he meant to keep it that way.

Hawkeye came through over the weekend, pulling the necessary strings to get a security and surveillance system team there to install the equipment at no charge to the youth center. Now, Will had the ability to observe all doors and main floor windows. An empty office was allocated to him for the monitoring system to be set up in for his use. Jules couldn't believe all of this was done before the first teen entered the center after school let out that day. Therefore, the kids had no reason to suspect the building was any different than it was the last time they were there.

"You're amazing, Will. It's like you speak the words and it happens."

"Don't go singing my praises yet. This operation isn't over."

"I have full faith in you." She touched his arm and smiled before turning and walking away.

He wished she hadn't said that. He felt like when people put their faith in others it was just setting them up for failure, something was always bound to go wrong 99.9 percent of the time. He wasn't a pessimist, not by a longshot. He'd missed enough foul shots in a tight basketball game to know that when the team was counting on him, it didn't always go his way. But things were different in the Army Rangers and working with the Brotherhood Protectors. It was teamwork that counted and maybe being a one man crew on this assignment had him feeling a little in left field, afraid of letting Jules down.

Or maybe you don't want to fall from the pedestal she's put you on, bro.

That thought shook him for a moment. Why should he care what she thought of him? He was her protector. He was here to do a job and that was to keep her safe, no matter what the cost or the outcome. Besides, he wasn't called Loverboy for nothing. He had a reputation of flirting with the ladies and leaving them in his wake before they knew what had hit them. He wasn't ready to settle down and he sure didn't plan on making the mistake of letting this assignment change him.

Will headed to Jules' office and unlocked the door with the set of keys the janitor had given him to all the rooms. Will wanted to make sure that the monitoring system in her office was set up exactly the way he wanted to pick up the best video and sound when necessary without her being self-conscious when talking with others. He made a cup of coffee for himself while he was there in the event she returned before he finished, but she didn't.

He returned to his office and checked the monitors, pleased with what he was seeing: teens actively using the center. He settled in his chair and sipped his coffee, opened up his laptop and began typing up a report on the day's events. He was typing mid-sentence when he heard Jules voice come over one of the monitor speakers. Looking up, he saw she'd entered her office and was talking to someone who hadn't come into view of the camera yet. He typed on the monitor's keyboard, switching camera angles to get a different look at the office and saw it was Rodrigo. Interesting. He adjusted the volume in the room so he could better hear what was being said.

"So what you want, Ms. Jules? I got peeps to hang with."

"I'm sure you do, but I wanted to have a chat, get caught up. It's been a week or so since we did that I believe."

Will could see she was flipping through her desk calendar and she stopped on a page. "Three weeks actually. Longer than normal. I'm sorry I let time slip by me like this. I do apologize.

"No need, Ms. Jules. All is good." Rodrigo leaned back, slouching in the chair, and spread his legs as wide as possible.

She sat back in her chair and smiled at him. "Is that right? Why don't you give me a little recap of what is good? Like those new shoes."

"Oh these. My boy Antonio gave me these for my birthday. Kinda sweet of him, don't you agree?"

"Antonio? I don't believe I know him."

"You wouldn't. He doesn't hang here."

She nodded. "Does he drive a car?"

Rodrigo shrugged. "Sometimes I guess. He's old enough."

Will shook his head at the smug, smoothness of this punk kid, but Jules didn't let it bother her. It was a good thing because if he was talking to him he'd have pulled him up by the shirt front by now and shook some of that smugness off him.

"Do you know where I live, Rodrigo?"

"What?" The kid sat up straight, dropping his leg to floor. "Why'd you ask that?"

"Because I thought I saw you in my neighborhood yesterday." Jules leaned forward across her desk. "In fact, I'm sure we made eye contact. Didn't we?"

Shit!

When did this happen? How had he missed it? Why hadn't she told him about seeing Rodrigo? Will thought there was a clear line of communication between him and Jules, but obviously he had been wrong.

Rodrigo shook his head. "You musta been imagining things, Ms. Jules."

"Don't lie to me, Rodrigo. It was you. Same shoes. Same bandana. Same eyes. I want to know was it a fluke that you were in my neighborhood or were you there because I was almost hit by a car."

The kid glared at her for a few moments.

"I'd been to see this girl and was headed to the 'L' when it happened. I saw it was you and had to make sure you were okay. You know how we all feel about you, Ms. Jules. You're the greatest. This place wouldn't be the same if something happened to you."

Jules leaned back in her chair. "Thank you for answering my question fully. Was that so hard to tell me why you were there? Did you think I'd be upset with your explanation?"

Rodrigo shrugged.

"So, tell me about this girl? I assume she doesn't go here either. How'd you meet? Is she cute? I'm sure she is if she caught your eye."

"You know me, Ms. Jules. I never kiss and spread the word."

"Yeah, Rodrigo. I know you."

Will shook his head. Jules couldn't let the kid off that easy. And she surely couldn't believe that he was really in her neighborhood seeing a girl that he wouldn't name the same day she was almost hit by a car, could she?

"So what else has been going on? I'm curious how the gang situation we've been discussion is going. When we last spoke you were being pressed to join. Has that changed?"

"It's the same song and dance, Ms. Jules. Nothing has changed. The leaders have made it clear I have until I turn seventeen to make it official or I'll die a slow Cobra death."

Rodrigo shook his head, shifted in the chair, and then Will heard a nervous chuckle.

"Yeah, you're not all cool and down with it as you'd like everyone to think, are you buddy?" Will muttered.

"It doesn't have to be that way, Rodrigo. I can get you help. I've found a good connection now. Someone that can help."

"How?"

There was silence for a moment or two.

He got to his feet. "That's what I thought. You never have an answer for me when I ask you that. I'll take my chances with the Twin Cobras. At least if I join them I know what I'm getting into. I have a chance at living."

"Don't go." She stood. "I can't answer your questions because I don't know *how*. I just know that I can get you help. There is a way out. You don't have to join the gang. And you won't have to die by not joining them."

"Keep believing that, Ms. Jules. Keep believing that. I'm outta here."

Rodrigo left her office, closing the door in his wake. Jules hung her head, balled her fists and pounded them on her desk. When she looked up, something glistened on her cheek, but she brushed it away quickly and sat back down, getting back to work.

Will turned the volume off and minimized the screen shot of her office, going back to typing his report. However, it was hard to concentrate on the subject when all he could think about was one, ways to keep Rodrigo out of the Twin Cobra gang without him getting killed and two, how to broach the subject with Jules if he came up with a solution if she didn't ask him for help.

. . .

BY THE TIME Will and Jules reached her apartment that evening, he'd received an encrypted email from Hawkeye on his phone with the camera footage of the street where Jules' hit and run almost happened the day before. "I've got something I need to take care of before dinner. Do you mind?" he asked.

"No. Go ahead. I'm still trying to decide on what to make. Any suggestions?"

"I'm easy to please."

"That's not really helpful," she called before he disappeared in his room.

He sat his tactical bag on the bed and got out his laptop, opened it up, and logged into the secured line to download the encrypted email so he could watch the footage. In the message, Hawkeye said a trace on the license plate was already in progress, as well as facial recognition on the two suspects. It sounded like there wasn't much he needed to do, but he watched the video footage anyway. He was amazed how clear of a shot into the car the camera angle had gotten on the two suspects. They had picked the worst spot on the street to park.

He took a few screen captures, then cropped the photos before going back into the kitchen to ask Jules if she recognized the two guys.

She slowly looked at each one. "No. But can you zoom in on what is hanging around that one's neck. It looks like it says something."

Will sat his laptop down on the kitchen counter and switched back to the original screen capture. The image was blurry, but he looked at the video until he found a clearer shot of it, snapped a screen shot, and zoomed in.

"Antonio." Will pointed a finger at the screen. "Doesn't it look like Antonio is saying to you?"

"Bingo," she said, her bottom lip trembled. "That's Rodrigo's boy who gave him the new shoes."

"Okay." Will nodded. "Are you certain these two weren't the guys that ran out of the Pied Piper on Friday night?"

"They're too thin, not rough around the edges enough. These boys like to act tough like Rodrigo does, but if you can crack their outer shell you'll find a heart of gold."

"You can tell all of that by looking at them?"

"A youth counselor worth a grain of salt knows how to read a young person on first glance."

He whistled, closing his laptop. "I wouldn't have wanted you to have been my counselor back in the day."

Jules quirked a grin, pursing her lips in the process, trying not to break out into a smile.

"I'll give Hawkeye a heads up that we've identified Antonio, but we only know his first name. We'll see what lead we can get back on him. I'm sure he's in the system for some petty theft or larceny."

She slowly nodded. "Wait. Do you think they were intentionally trying to hit me yesterday?"

"It sure looked like it, the way they peeled out of there and didn't stop."

"But your security footage from the area shops didn't show Rodrigo in the car at all, did it?"

"No."

"I didn't tell you yesterday, but when you were knocked out, I saw Rodrigo in the crowd of by-standers. I questioned him today and he claimed he had no idea he was in my neighborhood but was here seeing a girl he's interested in. I didn't fully believe him, but who knows, maybe he was telling the truth. Maybe he was here meeting up with a girl and his gang friends were here to pick him up. And for whatever reason they decided to take off like a bat out of hell while I was running across the street."

Will was glad to hear she hadn't been so gullible to buy Rodrigo's spiel earlier today. He was also glad she had come clean with him about seeing the teen in the crowd yesterday. It was good to know she wasn't intentionally keeping secrets from him, even if she had delayed telling him about it for over twenty-four hours. He wasn't going to make an issue out of it because it hadn't put her in danger and if he did, she might refrain from telling him pertinent information that he did need to know.

"That is one theory. Another is they could have received a call from their leader telling them to report to their hangout pronto. Or they'd been given orders if they saw you to give you a good scare because you've been talking to Rodrigo about not joining the gang. Who knows why they did it? We could spend hours talking about it and come up with a thousand reasons, or we can let the police handle it." He picked up his laptop. "My main concern is whether there's anything else that happened while I was knocked out yesterday that you haven't told me?"

"You moaning like a little boy?" she asked, her brows arching.

Her lighter tone told him she was making it up. He remembered enough of the incident that he was pretty sure that he hadn't moaned. He might have grunted when he hit the ground with a thud, or even when the back of her head butted him in the mouth, but he *definitely* hadn't moaned.

"If I had." He shot back not wanting her to think she was getting anywhere with him.

"I guess you'll never know."

He reached out and touched her on the arm. "It's okay to be scared by all of this, Jules. I would be if it were happening to me. A gang like the Twin Cobras taking notice of you for messing with one of their recruits is one thing, but we have no idea if they know you are a witness of the robbery and shooting at the Pied Piper also. That puts you in double jeopardy."

She took in a deep breath. "Thanks for reminding me, Will."

CHAPTER 7

THE NEXT FEW days Jules was always aware of her surroundings no matter if she was alone in her office at the youth center or at her apartment with Will. She couldn't relax. Not after he told her she was in double jeopardy with the Twin Cobras. He didn't know that for sure, but the possibility was high that her life was in danger if they learned she was trying to persuade Rodrigo against joining them. Even more if they learned she had witnessed gang members going to and fleeing from the Pied Piper on Friday night. The last thing she wanted was for anyone, especially Rodrigo, getting wind of that. He might let it slip to his boy Antonio in general conversation.

She knew it wasn't good to get herself all worked up over what ifs, but Will had made valid points. She'd tossed and turned most of Monday night thinking about them. She tried her best to keep her anxiety to herself and it appeared Will hadn't picked up on it as the week passed, but when she tried calling Colleen again without getting an answer Wednesday morning before they left for the youth center, she lost it.

She marched into the living room where Will was having his coffee and reading email. "I want to talk to Commander Burns."

"Okay." He looked up at her. "What about?"

"My friend Colleen. She still isn't answering her phone. I know something isn't right. She'd have charged her phone by now if that's all that's wrong. She'd also have reached out to me for our mid-week chat. Carly would have too."

Will closed his laptop and put it beside him on the sofa. "Simone and Carly's protectors have probably told them to be careful about using their phones. But we need to talk about Colleen and the reason you haven't been able to reach her."

Spidery-fingers of tension crept up her spine along with a chill and it was hard for her to move, but she forced her legs to walk the short distance around the sofa so she could sit down beside him. "You have me freaking out right now, Will, you know that."

"I'm sorry. I've thought of a hundred different ways I could tell you and there is no easy way not to worry you, but let me make it clear she is alive. I would have told you all of this last night when I finished talking to Wyatt Kincaid, but you were already asleep and I didn't want to wake you."

"I appreciate your concern for my sleep. Now, who is Wyatt and what did he say?"

"The good news is he's Colleen's protector. The bad news is Colleen's phone was destroyed in the incident Friday night."

"Is that all, Will McLeod?" Jules punched him on the arm, hard and her voice escalated as she spoke. "You had me thinking something horrible had happened to her."

"Something did. While the robbery was going on in the bar, Colleen had gone to the ladies room. It appears someone followed and attacked her in the there."

"Oh…my…was she…was she…"

"No. Just beaten. Wyatt relayed that Colleen said the gunshot scared the attacker away before anything more could happen, but he ran off with her purse. It was later found in a dumpster down the street, all contents recovered, but her phone had been crushed, like it had been stomped on several times to crack the GPS tracking system in it."

"But Colleen? How is she doing? Can I go see her?" Jules jumped up off the sofa and began pacing. "Oh poor thing. She's the last one of us who dresses to attract a man. Do you know that?" Jules stopped in front of him for a moment, pivoted and headed back in the other direction. "I mean, I don't go out of my way to dress sexy like Simone. And we forced Carly to dress like something out of a Victoria's Secret catalog Friday night. Bought her the outfit and shoes to go with it. But otherwise, she's rather on the conservative side herself. Colleen wears sedate skirts and button up blouses. She pulls her hair back in a ponytail."

"But what if the guy had a naughty librarian fetish? Clothes have nothing to do with it. He'd attacked Colleen even if she had been wearing jeans and a baggy sweatshirt if she were there at the same time and same place."

Jules planted her hands on her hips and took a deep breath. Then looked at him for a few seconds. "When can I go see her?"

"I wish I could take you to her, but she's checking out of the hospital today and from what Wyatt said, he's taking her to a safe house to recoup. Her parents have been arguing about which one should take her home with them and it has been non-stop bickering between them since Saturday."

"Of course they would." Jules sat back down. "It's always about their needs, which one of them is in control more than what Colleen needs. I'm surprised those two can even stand to see their daughter each week for brunch, but they do it. I'm sure it's another ploy to see which one can outdo the other."

"That sounds screwed up to me."

"Oh it is, but Colleen thinks her parents are so cool to be friends after the divorce. She can't see what they really are doing under her nose, bless her."

"Let me put a call through to Wyatt and see if you can speak to Colleen for a few minutes before we leave for work this morning. I can at least do that for you."

She reached out a hand and placed it on his. "Thank you, Will. It means so much that you'd do that for me."

He pulled out his phone and looked up Wyatt's number in his contacts. The line was answered after three rings.

"What's up, Will?" Wyatt said.

"I was hoping Colleen might be okay with speaking to a friend this morning?"

"Sure. Hang on a moment. Hey Colleen. I have a call for you. Are you interested in taking it?"

Will didn't wait for Colleen to come on the line, he handed the phone to Jules.

"Colleen?" Jules said into the phone as soon as she put it to her ear.

"Jules?"

Jules closed her eyes for a second then opened them again. "It's wonderful to hear from you. I hope you aren't upset with me for not calling sooner. I just found out where you were."

"It's okay. I've not felt like talking anyway. It hurt to speak at first and I didn't feel up to it really, but I had to talk with a therapist for evaluation before they'd let me leave here. How are you?"

"I'm good. I wish I hadn't left the bar when I did on Friday. If I hadn't then I would have been inside with the rest of you when all of this went down."

"No, Jules. You were where you needed to be to see what you saw. Besides, you needed to take care of the kids at the youth center. You didn't need to be tied up with this mess to the extent Carly and Simone are."

"How exactly are they involved? You seem to know so much more than I do, Colleen? How is that?"

"They escaped from their protectors and came here on Saturday to see me."

"They what?" Jules looked at Will, wondering what Brand and Donovan must look like if her two friends had disregarded their protector's size and made a break for it to go see Colleen anyway.

"I haven't heard from or seen them since, so I'm sure they've been chastised severely for it. Wyatt claimed they wouldn't be able to sit down for a while after the chewing out they'd receive. Commander Burns was not happy with Simone, but you know what lip she has on her at times."

Jules nodded. "It sounds like that whatever happened inside the bar on Friday didn't change her any."

"No worries on that front. She was making lewd comments to Carly about getting her protector where she wanted him before the week was out. If I heard her, I'm sure the men did too."

Jules giggled, looking at Will. He tapped his index finger on the face of his watch so she nodded in understanding. "I have to go now, Colleen, but it has been wonderful talking to you. I know it will be a while before we can talk again so you take care and know that I love you, my friend."

"You too, Jules. I'll see you soon."

The line went dead. Jules slowly lowered the phone from her ear and stared at the black screen. She didn't make a move for a good minute or two, then she finally handed the phone back to Will. "I don't think I want to go to work today."

"Why not?" he asked, sounding shocked by her declaration.

"This week has been a little too much emotionally for me."

Will shook his head. "That's the very reason you need to go work. You need to stay busy or you'll be idle with have too much time on your hands to dwell on everything that has happened."

She groaned. "Why do you have to always be right?"

"It's part of my job."

"No, it isn't."

"How do you know? It could be."

She stuck her tongue out at him.

He laughed. Then he tapped the face of his watch again. "We better get going. We've already missed our normal 'L' stop."

She sighed, went to her room and got her satchel, not really feeling it today. And that was so unlike her. She loved going to the center. She lived for those kids. Today, she just wanted to stay in her room and put her PJs back on and crawl under the covers and cry for Colleen. What horror she must have gone through alone in that restroom at the Pied Piper and then the aftermath, not knowing if her identity had been stolen when her purse was taken. Not to mention not knowing if her apartment had been robbed since the perp had her address and keys. Only to find out later everything was good that the only thing she lost was her phone.

Jules knew she had gotten off lucky so far. All she'd had happen was someone tried to run her down in a crosswalk. That seemed nothing at all to what Colleen had been through.

"Jules?" Will called.

She sank to the floor in front of her bed and pulled her knees up to her chest, resting her forehead on her knees. She really didn't want to leave the apartment today even if the kids needed her. She'd been serious when she said she needed a personal day. Now that she knew what had happened with Colleen she needed to know about Carly and Simone. What had happened to them once they left the hospital after seeing Colleen? What punishment had their protectors bestowed on them? What trauma, if any, had each sustained at the bar or afterward as a repercussion of the shooting?

WILL WAITED, but when Jules didn't respond, he walked to her room and found Jules huddled at the end of her bed. This was not a good sign. Was he wrong to make her go into work today? Maybe she really did need to take a personal day. No. He thought back to everything Wyatt had told him about PTSD cases and he knew the best medicine for Jules was to keep her active, whether she wanted to follow his directive or not.

He cleared his throat to get her attention, but she didn't look up or acknowledge that he'd come into her room. "I can tell you're upset. Is it okay if I hug you?"

"Hug me?" Jules' head finally popped up and she looked at him. "Do you always ask a woman before you do that?"

"No, but with you I've found you push me away when I attempt to console you."

"I don't do that…oh, I guess I did on Sunday when I burst into tears, but that was only because I'd gotten my emotions in check and if you'd touched me I was afraid I'd crumbled into despair again."

"Fair enough, but I didn't want to overstep my bounds with you this time. I'm here to protect you, not distress you. Right now you look like you've been carrying the weight of the world on your shoulders all week and my letting you call Colleen didn't help. It only made it worse."

"No. No. I needed to talk to her. But now I'm worried about Carly and Simone, wondering what ordeal they've been facing this week while I've been pretty much living my life as normal."

"I wouldn't call this week normal." Will sank down beside her on the floor. "You've had a total stranger living in your apartment with you. Is that normal?"

"You're not a stranger. You're my new friend." She reached for his hand. "I couldn't have gotten through this without you."

"I'm glad you feel that way. So listen to me when I tell you that you need to relax a little, Jules. Don't worry so much about the things you can't control. Remember Carly and Simone are not alone in this. They have Brand and Donovan to protect them. A DEVGRU SEAL and a Marine. Both highly qualified men to protect and serve."

She slowly gave him a smirk. "And what are you, McLeod? An Army Ranger with a deathly blow to the heart? Is that why they call you Loverboy, because you leave women swooning in your wake?""

He chuckled, wrapping an arm around her shoulders. "You know Gentry, even when you are down you try to find humor in the darkest moments."

"You can thank my gramps for that. He always said laughter was the best medicine."

"And single-malt scotch."

"Ummm…that sure would hit the spot right now. I'm sure I have a bottle in the cabinet. I always keep more than one in the apartment." She started to get to her feet, but he trapped her by wrapping his other arm around her.

"I think scotch drinking can wait a few more hours. It's not even half-past eight. Surely you don't mean to drink and go into the youth center today."

"I don't plan to go to the youth center at all."

He gave her a level look. "We already discussed this. You need to go to work."

"No I don't."

"Jules, what if this afternoon is the day that Rodrigo comes to your office needing your help and you aren't there?"

She shook her head. "We both know Rodrigo will do whatever he wants to do. He's not going to come looking for me today or tomorrow or the day after to help him out. He's made that perfectly clear. He's going to join the gang because he believes gang life is the evil he knows."

Will leaned his head back against the bed. He couldn't believe he was hearing defeat in her voice. What in the world had taken her down this path today?

He looked down at her. "I'm not giving up that easy. Deep down I don't think you are ready to give up on him either. It's just this dark funk you are in today."

She started to protest, but before she could speak he pulled her to him and captured her mouth with his own, stopping her words from coming. Instead, he heard a muffled moan escape her throat as she twisted in his arms to face him more, responding to him.

When they finally broke apart he stared at her and she stared at him until their breathing returned to normal. Neither said a word for several minutes.

"What made you do that?" Her question came out in a rush and she flushed, breaking her gaze with him.

"You have the prettiest mouth. It cried to be kissed. Sitting this close to you I couldn't ignore the temptation anymore. Has anyone ever told you that before?"

"Oh, you have got to have a better line than that one."

A line? Did she think he was trying to put a move on her?

He scooted a few inches away and got up. If he'd meant it as a come on she'd have known it. "I'll be waiting for you in the living room when you are ready to go to work."

"I told you I'm not going."

"You are and that's final."

JULES SAT THERE FUMING. She balled her firsts, hitting them on the floor, before releasing them. Why was he being so obstinate? Why couldn't he let her stay home and sulk? She didn't like the tone he'd taken with her like she was a child being ordered around. She slowly got to her feet and went into her bathroom checking her hair to see if she needed to comb or restyle it, but it was coifed perfectly. Her lipstick on the other hand needed to be touched up because it was a little smudged from his kiss.

"All day wear my foot," she muttered, capping the lid back on the tube after reapplying it.

Satisfied, she joined him in the living room with her satchel slung across her shoulder. She walked to the kitchen and took out their lunches. "I'm ready when you are."

"I believe I know why you're feeling the way you are today."

"You do?"

"You went from worrying over the funding for the youth center, to the bar shooting, and then almost getting hit by that car. Not to mention your concern for Rodrigo and of course, your friends. Let's agree to shelve your friends because they each have a protector looking after them like me. They're in safe hands. I can guarantee that."

She slowly drew in a jagged breath. "Okay."

"Now, Rodrigo is a punk ass teen who thinks he's invincible just like I was at that age. I know the type. I'm working on finding him a safe out, one that will fit his interests. A basketball camp that would get him away from here for the summer, for starters. It will teach him some discipline without him realizing it as well as put distance between him and the Twin Cobras."

This news made her smile. She couldn't believe he'd been thinking about how to help Rodrigo. She hadn't even broached the subject with him. He was a really awesome guy and yet she'd just accused him of trying to put moves on her because of that kiss. That wonderful kiss.

Real smooth, Gentry.

She'd also been pissy with him for trying to

keep her mind off of her sorrows all because he wanted her to stay busy today. Yet, she'd been making a stink over it.

Again, not good.

"I'm sorry about before."

"It's not totally okay, but it's forgotten. Let's go or we'll miss the next 'L.'"

CHAPTER 8

JULES FOUND that once she got to work and settled into her routine that she was fine. It was mainly leaving her apartment and getting to work that had been the biggest hurdle for her today. She still thought about Carly and Simone off and on as the morning went by, but she knew Will was right—they were in capable hands with their protectors. She also spend some time thinking back to his surprise kiss and she decided it was best not to dwell on it, because if she did it might make their relationship turn awkward and she didn't want that.

Will dropped by her office at lunch and they ate their sandwiches together. At first, they were eating in silence and she knew that couldn't go on. There had to be something they could talk about.

"You were talking about Rodrigo going away for

the summer to get away from gang life. What about when he returns?"

"I'm still working out the details on that with Hawkeye. Ideally it would be good if he and his family could start fresh in a new location, so he isn't near any connection to the Twin Cobras, but I know that would be too disruptive to uproot them. So another alternative will need to be considered."

"That's not a bad idea really."

Will's brows arched. "What do you know about his home life? What kind of neighborhood do they live in?"

She shrugged. "I know his parents are older. When they came to a family function at the center, I mistook them for his grandparents. They had him later in life. Both are hard workers and their jobs keep them away from home long hours. Rodrigo talks about how he wishes his mom would find a different job so she could spend more time at home, so when she is there she isn't always working too. When he talks about her he mentions that she works too much. He wants to make things easier on them both."

"That's good. That's real good. It gives us leverage to get to him." Will leaned back in his chair. "If we can show him how he can make their lives better by leaving the area, maybe even offer his dad a better job in the new place, which could sweeten the deal. One that would pay enough so the mom wouldn't have to work at all or as many hours a week if she felt she still needed to work outside the home."

"I'm liking this. But the operative word is 'if' we can get the family to agree to move."

"I believe if you were to reach out to the parents, explain to them about the gang recruiting their son they'd be open to it."

"Their only child," she pointed out.

"Their only son. Their one chance to carry on the family name."

"Okay. You don't have to sell me on it. I'm with you one-hundred percent."

Will nodded. "Yeah. I think that is a good angle to go for. I run it by Hawkeye before we act. Maybe he'll have some additional suggestions for us on what we can offer the family, like housing opportunities, job placements. Until we have it all worked out, let's keep it hush-hush."

"Of course."

"Great. See you a little later." He took a few steps toward the door and turned around. "Oh, you haven't seen the day janitor around have you? He hasn't poked his head out of his hole today and I really need to his help on a project."

She laughed in spite of herself.

"Eddie is a nice guy. You shouldn't make fun of him even if he does prefer to stay downstairs the majority of the time. I'm sure he is around some-where. Keep looking for him."

"I wasn't making fun. I just mean if he *is* here, I haven't seen him yet. I've been all over the building a couple of times already, but I'll look again. I'm sure I just missed him."

After Will left, Jules got to thinking about where Eddie could be. He wasn't one of the people she normally saw often in the building, but he was always there when you needed him. So she left her office and went down the hall to check with a colleague to see if she'd seen him pass by that morning.

"I haven't, Jules. Why don't you ask our new security guy? I'm sure he has seen him on his cameras."

"Sure. Thanks."

She left it at that not wanting to alarm her coworker if there wasn't a reason. Likewise, she didn't think it was a good idea to go to another office on down the hall and inquire with another colleague the same thing. If she did that, then someone might become alarmed.

Instead, she went back to her office and put Eddie out of her mind while she prepared for her group activity with the junior high girls that afternoon.

. . .

WILL STOPPED by the administrative office after leaving Jules' office to make sure that Eddie had reported to work today, which he had. Then Will proceeded to do another walkthrough of the entire facility, stopping by Eddie's workroom. But the man wasn't there and it didn't look like he'd been there all day either, which didn't make sense if he reported to work. His janitor's cart sat in the corner, so that meant he wasn't out cleaning an area of the building.

Returning to his security room, Will pulled the video feed for the past six hours down in the corridor where Eddie's workroom was located and watched it. He fast forwarded through footage of empty space until it picked up on someone in the area. Then he slowed down and watched. He saw Eddie stop at his workshop and unlock the door, but then two young men came from the shadows like they had been waiting for him. This puzzled Will because he'd made sure the facility was secure on Monday when the security system was put in and no one could get into the facility without a key. Unless there was a set of keys to the youth center in the wrong hands.

Will typed a few keys on the keyboard so the footage would rewind and watched as Eddie came into view again, and slowed it down as the two young men came out of the shadows. There wasn't audio downstairs because it hadn't seemed necessary to have it all over the building. Just in Jules' office. Eddie left and went with them. Will stopped the footage, jotted down the time stamp from the camera downstairs and tried to find footage from the side exits that matched the same time. He finally found Eddie and the two young men heading out to the small parking lot where Eddie parked his old truck. He shook the young men's hands and jumped in his truck, leaving the parking lot as fast as his truck could travel.

Will zoomed in on the truck's license plates and jotted those down before calling Hawkeye directly.

"Commander Burns."

"Hawkeye. It's McLeod. I need to run an APB on a plate. Our janitor mysteriously left the facility today soon after arriving and hasn't been seen since. I want to make sure there isn't foul play involved."

"I can't go issuing APBs on vehicles without good reason, McLeod. Besides, I'm already tied up with another case at the moment. You have to give me more reason than a janitor leaving work suddenly."

"He didn't report to the administration that he was leaving. Don't you find that odd? Also, there were two unidentified young men that approached him in the building before he left. They shouldn't have been able to have gotten into the youth center unless someone let them in."

"Did this janitor appear in distress when he left?" Hawkeye questioned.

"Not really. He shook the young men's hands before he got in his truck and high-tailed it out of the parking lot."

"So you have only an assumption that foul-play is going on. I'm willing to go out on a limb within reason, but not on this one. Find more reason or cause and I'll do it. I have to go. I've arrived at the scene."

"I understand. But Hawkeye, Eddie just isn't any janitor. He lives to serve these kids at the center. He's like Jules in that way. I don't think he'd have left here unless something was wrong. Maybe not with him but someone in his family."

"I get it, McLeod. I wish I could do more, but without proof I can't."

Will ended the call, not happy with the outcome, but he saw Hawkeye's point. He took a few moments to merge the video footage from the two difference cameras into one clip before he did a review of other camera recordings to see if he could pick up how the two young men gained access into the building.

A couple of hours had passed by the time he finished reviewing footage. Then he accessed live feed of students approaching the building that afternoon. He saw students running and he heard screaming. Then he saw a couple of boys carrying a kid between them toward the center.

Will grabbed his phone and his tactical bag and left his office, pulling the door closed behind him. He was outside in seconds accessing the situation.

"What's happened?" he asked as other administrators and Jules exited the building.

"Devon was jumped and beaten," a girl explained.

"These two guys came out of nowhere and attacked him," another girl said.

"Did you see if Devon said or did anything to provoke the guys?" Will asked.

"No, man. Devon didn't say nothin'," a guy in the crowd said. "Those guys are gang bangers. They had a job to do. It didn't matter who they jumped as long as they jumped someone."

"He's hurt pretty badly, Ms. Jules," one the boy's carrying Devon said.

"Let's take him inside. The front office has a couch that is the closest spot. Follow Clara, she'll let you into the office," Jules instructed. "I'll call an ambulance and be right there."

"We're scared, Ms. Jules," two girls said at the same time, hugging Jules around the waist. She wrapped her arm around one as she tried to talk on her cellphone requesting the ambulance.

Will helped the other administrators usher the teens into the gymnasium where they could all be contained and he could assess who saw what. A sign-in sheet was sent around to know which teens were there that day. Then they were divided into groups and stationed in the gym with different youth center councilors for activities.

Once Will saw that everything was under control, he went to check on the injured boy in the front office. That is where he found Jules, holding the boy's hand and talking to him, reassuring him that everything was going to be okay.

Jules looked up at him, said something to the boy before coming over to talk to him. She let out a deep breath and planted her hands on her hips. "To think I didn't want to come in today. I'd have never forgiven myself if I hadn't been here today and this happened."

"We can't know when bad things are going to happen, if we did we'd stop then before they did."

"I've called the police about this," she said. "I hope you aren't upset, but it's policy here. I've also called Devon's parents."

"I'm not upset. I was debating it myself, but after I called Hawkeye about Eddie I was hesitant."

"Eddie?"

"It's probably nothing, like Hawkeye said, but I have footage of him leaving shortly after he arrived his morning. Two young men met him downstairs and walked out with him. He took off in a hurry."

Jules made a pained face and raised her left

hand, resting the tips of her index and middle finger in the middle of her forehead. "His wife. She has a terminal illness. I don't know why I didn't think of it earlier when you mentioned you couldn't find him today. I don't know if that is the reason, but it could have been."

"He didn't report he was leaving."

She dropped her arm and looked him square in the eye. "If it was your dying wife and you had only so long to get there would you think to do that?"

Will looked down at the floor as the sound of sirens penetrated through the stone walls of the building. "No. I guess I wouldn't. But let's not forget that we are only speculating why he left. There could be another reason especially after two unidentified young men jumped Devon as the students were headed here after school."

"They weren't unidentified. You heard Troy. He said they were gang bangers. New recruits here to do a job. To find a target, any target, and get the job done."

Will sucked in a breath. "I stand corrected."

"Are we really going to argue over this?" Jules asked him.

"We aren't arguing. We're having a discussion."

"If sounds life arguing to me," Devon slurred from the couch.

Jules left Will and went back over to where the

teen lay. "I'm sorry if we were too loud, we're just worried about you and the safety of everyone else."

Will thought for a moment, unwilling to give up that easy that he was right on this matter. There was something that just didn't feel right about the way Eddie had left the building. Call it intuition or suspicion, but he needed to make sure to cover all basis. He sat down his tactical bag and pulled out his laptop.

"Devon, I want you to take a look at this image for me and tell me if you recognize these guys. Were they the two that beat you up?"

Jules helped the boy to a sitting position so he could see the computer screen better since one eye was partially swollen closed.

The teen nodded and pointed at the screen. "If them."

Will looked up at Jules and then back at Devon. "Thank you."

The door to the office opened and Sergeant TJ entered followed by two EMTs. "Trouble seems to follow you, McLeod."

"Don't I know it?" Will shook his hand and showed him his computer screen. "Devon just identified his attackers as these two who entered the premises this morning and caused our janitor to leave soon after he arrived."

"Well, it looks like you have redeemable qualities after all. Shoot me that footage and I'll take it from here."

"An adult needs to go with him. I'll ride to the hospital with Devon," Jules said. "Let me get my satchel."

She wasn't gone long until they heard screaming coming down the hallway. Will and TJ took off running in the direction of her office. When they reached it, they found her standing to the side of her desk pointing at her chair where two baby Cobras were hissing away.

"Holy Mother," TJ said. "How'd those get in here?"

"Jules, you did lock your door earlier?" Will questioned.

"Of course. I had to unlock it to get inside."

Will swore under his breath. "Then it's as I suspected this morning. Someone who shouldn't has a set of keys to this building."

"What do you mean?" TJ asked.

"It's the only way to explain how the two who attacked Devon also got into the youth center this morning to talk to our janitor."

"That's all fine and good, but while you hash this out I need to get my bag so I can ride to the hospital with Devon."

"Where's it at?" TJ asked.

"Under my desk, in the opening where my chair slides into. There is a hook I hang it on so it doesn't have to sit on the floor. You can't see it from here."

"Then we need to pull your desk away from the chair so we can get your bag." TJ looked at Will. "Don't you think that should work?"

"Are you sure?" Jules asked. "It's a pretty heavy desk. Sometimes I think it must have been constructed out of steel or something when I've tried to push it back an inch."

"How hard can it be?" TJ moved the guest chair out of the way so he could try to pull the desk forward. He tugged, but the desk wouldn't budge. "Will, give me a hand."

Will got into the action and the two strained, but the desk wasn't going anywhere. "Is it bolted to the floor?"

"Oh good grief!" Jules squatted down and looked around the corner to see if she saw any prongs on the inside opening with bolts that she hadn't noticed before. The Cobras hissed at her and she pulled away fast before she could reach for her satchel.

"We need to get rid of those."

"I'll call animal control," TJ said. "I might not be able to move the desk, but I can do that for you."

Clara showed up at her open doorway. "Jules, the EMTs are ready to leave. Are you going with them or not?"

"Not," Will answered for her. "Do you mind

going with Devon? There's been a development that requires she stay here."

"Of course. Do you hear hissing?"

"It's my new pet Cobra snakes someone dropped off in my chair," Jules explained.

Clara's eyes grew large. "Oh. I. See. Yes. You do need to stay here. Bless you, Jules. Stay safe."

"I have called Devon's parents so they will meet you at the hospital," Jules added.

"I'll keep him in my care until they do."

"I've also called a patrol unit to meet the ambulance at the hospital to make sure none of the Twin Cobras show up there to do anymore harm," TJ added.

"Thank you," Clara said before she hurried away.

When she left, Jules walked over to Will and punched him in chest with her index finger. "I am more than capable of answering for myself, thank you very much. I know I cannot leave here under the circumstances. I'd be putting Devon and everyone else in that hospital at risk if I did."

"Now Jules, calm down."

"No. I won't calm down." She poked him again in the chest. "I have every right to be upset with you. I appreciate you're here to protect me, but I don't need you speaking for me. Is that clear, Mr. McLeod?" When she finished, she poked him one last time before she stalked from her office.

TJ whistled. "Is she always so high-spirited?"

"Today has been an unusually emotional day for her. She's usually the one in control and she hasn't been since last Friday. So cut her some slack. I'm not making it easier on her when I try to take care of her. She's not had anyone to do that in years. I just keep forgetting."

"Isn't that your job as her protector?" TJ asked.

"Yes."

TJ shook his head. "Glad I'm not you."

Will grinned, wondering where Jules had gone off to. He didn't like the idea that he didn't know where she was when someone had access to the building despite his efforts to secure it.

His cellphone rang and he answered. "McLeod here."

"It's Hawkeye. I just heard over the police radio about what's gone down over at the youth center. Is everything under control? Do you need extra backup? I also heard that Animal Control has been called in."

"The Twin Cobras left a calling card. We're waiting for those to be picked up now."

"That's twice they've struck today," Hawkeye said.

"Twice?"

"Yeah. My other case. Has the janitor showed back up?"

"Not yet. Jules says his wife is terminally ill. I'm

not sure if she is in hospice care or home, but the two young men that were here this morning are the same ones that attacked the teen this afternoon. They are associated with the gang."

"Sorry I didn't listen to you earlier. Maybe this could have been avoided."

"No. If they wanted to attack here today, they would have done it one way or another. The way I see it, they attacked Devon to get us out of the building, or at least Jules out of her office so they could leave the calling card to warn her what could happen if she didn't stop meddling in gang business."

"And how is she meddling?" Hawkeye asked.

"She's been trying to persuade one of their recruits to not join the gang. This was long before what happened on Friday night."

"Or could it be the reason the Twin Cobras hit the Pied Piper? Could the gang have gotten word from the kid at the youth center that Jules was going to be at the bar on Friday night? Is that the reason they decided to target it, but she'd already left by the time they struck? We haven't established a motive for why the gang was there. The one we've got in custody isn't talking. He lawyered up pretty quick but thankfully the judge denied bail."

"Those are all good questions that only my talking to Rodrigo will answer. And you know what Hawkeye, I just realized I haven't seen that kid today. He's always here after school. I need to go. I need to find where Jules went and make sure she is safe since she left my sight."

"I think I'm coming over even if you don't need backup. We may have a situation on our hands."

JULES CAME out of the ladies room feeling refreshed after splashing cool water on her face. She debated about going back to her office, but she wasn't ready to see Will just yet, so she headed to the gymnasium to check on her teens. As she drew closer she could hear laughter and talking coming from behind the double wooden doors.

"Oh hey, Ms. Jules," Rodrigo said, leaning against the wall of the corridor with one leg bent. He pushed away with his foot and came over to her. "I heard there was a ruckus right after everyone arrived. I missed it all. Had to stay after-school for detention today because of a squabble that disrupted class. The principal made us stay after school for an hour."

"Rodrigo, what am I going to do with you?" she said. "Shouldn't you have went on into the gym with everyone else?"

"I was in there, but I didn't see you. I wanted to make sure you were okay. Some of the girls were talking about how you were with the boy that got hurt."

"Thank you for always worrying about me, but I am fine. I did stay with Devon until the ambulance came." She smiled and reached out her hand to him. "Come, let's go into the gym with the others."

"Not yet, Ms. Jules. Can we talk? About what happened at school?"

"Of course. I always have time to talk when you have issues." She looked around for a place they could go and sit but there wasn't anywhere near them. "Let's go outside and sit under the tree on the bench. It's a pretty afternoon."

"Sure."

They took one of the side exits out near the small parking lot and walked over to where the bench was under the tree.

Rodrigo wasted no time diving into his problem. "The principal said if it happens again he's going to have to transfer me. I've been trying really hard to do right, but these other kids are always saying things disrespect ul and putting me and my friends down. Like they are so much better than we are and today it was all because of this new girl I like. One of them saw us holding hands in the hallway in between classes and started in on us."

"I see. How does that make her feel?"

"She hates it. She's afraid her family will hear of it and put a stop to us seeing each other because of the Twin Cobras. They wouldn't want her dating a gang member."

"Rodrigo, then shouldn't you take that into consideration before you join them? If you really like this girl? If you won't do it for yourself or your family, then consider what joining the gang will do for your relationship with her."

"I thought you'd say that." He stood and walked away from her toward the side street where the bus line dropped most of the student off at the center. "But it isn't that easy. I've been picked. And when you've been picked there is no turning back unless you do what they demand."

Jules followed him. "There has to be another way."

"There isn't. I'm sorry, Ms. Jules. I really am."

"Why are you sorry?"

CHAPTER 9

THE WORDS LEFT JULES' mouth as a black car pulled up and the back passenger door opened. Two guys jumped out and threw a sack over her head so fast she didn't have time to react before she was picked up and tossed into the trunk. Her hands were bound together in front of her, then someone else was tossed inside with her before she was left in total darkness when the trunk lid closed. Maybe it was everything that had happened in the last half-week, but she felt she had no fight in her to prevent this from happening. If this was the Twin Cobras come to get her, so be it. If they thought taking her was the answer to letting Rodrigo go free she'd let them take her. She was tougher than they knew. Will would come find her. Her cellphone was in her jeans pocket. If she could figure out a way to get her hands over to her pocket, perhaps she could work her fingers down the fabric opening enough to maneuver the phone up to call him so he could track her movements. But she'd have to be careful not to drop it or let it slide down her hip. If it did that she might not be able to figure out a way to get to it again.

The plan all seemed to work beautifully in her mind, but it didn't go so well when she tried executing it as the car began to move, bouncing along the uneven pavement, jostling her and her companion in the process. Maybe if she enlisted the other person's aid that would help. If the person was conscious. All she could hear was labored breathing near her ear and the crunching of gravel as the car obviously traveled the back streets away from the youth center.

"Rodrigo, is that you?" she whispered.

"Jules? Why are you whispering? They can't possibly hear us back here."

That wasn't Rodrigo's voice, but she knew it. Her brain rushed trying to process the timber until she placed it. "Eddie?"

"Yes. What's going on? Where are we?"

"I'm not sure what's going on, but we are in the trunk of a car. How long have you been with the Twin Cobras today? What made you leave the youth center this morning?"

"It was all a wild goose chase to get me to leave. Not sure why anyone would want to play a cruel joke on a man like that." He paused for a moment. "These two teens came telling me I needed to go see my wife immediately that she was about to pass. But when I got to the hospice facility she was the same as she was yesterday. I stayed with her for a while before leaving since I was there. When I came out I had a flat tire on my truck. So I set to fix it, bending down to take the lug nuts off. That's when this sack was put on my head and someone hit me from behind, knocking me out."

What reason did the Twin Cobras have for involving Eddie if all they wanted in the end was to get to her?

It didn't make sense at all.

"I'm sorry that happened, but we need to concentrate on what's happening to us right now. I think if we can work together we can get my phone out of my jeans pocket to make a call to Will. That open line should help him trace our location, if we can do it."

"My hands are bound behind my back," Eddie explained.

"Of course they would be," she grumbled. "Mine are in front, palms facing, because they threw me in first, then tied them."

"Sloppy, sloppy."

Jules giggled. "But it works to my advantage if I can just get my fingers to work right."

"What do you want me to do?"

"Kick out a taillight if you can. That could get the car pulled over."

"Good idea," Eddie said.

She heard movement beside her that sounded like he was rocking back and forth to roll away from her so he was on his right side, putting his left foot at the right height to do damage at the old Cadillac's taillight.

While he did that, she went to work trying to get her phone out of her pocket again. She almost had it when it began to ring. Her startled movement made the phone slip down in the pocket and she had to start anew trying to work her way to bring it out again.

"Get it or they'll hear it in the car," Eddie ordered.

"I'm trying, but it isn't easy." Jules gritted her teeth as she worked harder to fish her phone out of her pocket, finally bringing it out as the ringing ended. She laid the phone on her chest, giving a sigh of relief and noticed if she twisted her arms just so she bring her hands up to her face and push the sack up her face so she could breathe easier. Untwisting them she raised them naturally upward and was able to pull the sack with her thumbs further up her head. Satisfied that was enough to give her amble sight, she lowered her arms again and waited, hoping whoever had called would call back in a minute or two. She picked up the phone again so it was already in her hands when it rang again.

Eddie rolled toward her making her drop the phone before he rolled away again, giving a hard kick at the taillight. The sound of cracking plastic told of his success.

The phone landed with a little thud on the floorboard and began to ring. She rocked her body this time so she could turn onto her side and scoop up the phone before it stopped ringing. Swiping was more difficult than she imagined it would be. She tried with her pinky and finally got a firm swipe.

"Jules?"

"Will, don't hang up. Can you hear me?"

"Yes, I can hear you, but you sound muffled and far away. Where are you?"

"In the trunk of a car with Eddie." She twisted her arms to bring the phone closer to her mouth. "Is this better?"

"Much."

"It's an older model black Cadillac with a missing taillight. Eddie was able to kick it out. Sorry I can't give you more of a description. That is all I saw before a sack was pulled over my head and I was thrown in the trunk. It happened so fast I didn't have a chance to fight back."

"Are you hurt?"

"Not physically. My ego is a little bruised."

"Keep talking. Just a little more and your GPS signal should triangulate with a cell tower. Do you have a sense of which direction the car was headed when it left the center?"

"I believe it took side streets because I heard gravel crunching. That means were headed into a more residential area, away from downtown."

"That helps. Got your signal. You said Eddie is with you? Is he okay?"

"Yeah. He was tricked into leaving the center today. Long story."

"I'll be glad to hear it once we have you both back. Hang tight, don't end the call. Hawkeyes here I need to get him up to speed."

Jules straightened up, bumping her back against Eddie. "Sorry."

"No problem. We're packed in here like sardines."

"It's getting harder to breathe too," she said, closing her eyes. She started coughing. "Eddie, are you okay?"

WILL RODE with Hawkeye in the SUV cruiser, following the GPS signal to a part of town he had never been. It went deep into the residential area and then back out into a more deserted warehouse district near the waterfront. The sun was getting lower in the sky from the rear as they approached

the location where the GPS signal blinked on his laptop screen like a beacon.

Switching the app from the laptop to his phone, Will was ready to get out of the cruiser as soon as they stopped a good block from where the signal indicated was Jules' location.

"Let's stay together on this," Hawkeye said. "Don't go half-cocked and try to be the hero just because she's your assignment. Got it?"

"Of course. That's not my style. It's Don Juan's."

Hawkeye frowned as they stepped out of the vehicle like he didn't understand.

"Donovan."

"Oh, yeah. You guys have too many nicknames."

Will grinned. "Doesn't every brotherhood?"

TJ and two men dressed in street clothes joined them outside the cruiser. TJ introduced them as detectives from the gang violence division.

"Are we going in blind here?" Hawkeye asked.

"All our CI could tell us is they're in the building with the green double doors down the street," one of the detectives said.

"Hell, the GPS told us that much," Hawkeye said. "Your CI isn't living up to their end of the bargain if that is all they can provide."

"Or that's where they want us to think they are," the other detective said. "For all we know they may have popped the trunk and tossed the girl's cellphone in the warehouse when they realized she had it on her and was using it, then took off to another location in the car."

"It's a possibility," Will agreed. "But if I know Jules she made sure they didn't detect it if at all possible."

"That girl has tenacity. She'd do it too," TJ agreed.

"We're losing daylight, fellas," Hawkeye reminded them. "Let's split up. TJ, Harrison, O'Conner go around back and scope things out while McLeod and I go from the front." He motioned for his driver to lower the window. "Call for patrol back up in the area. No sirens or lights on approach."

"You got it, Commander."

The group went in their separate ways, Will and Hawkeye making sure to stay close to the buildings as they approached the double green doors. Will watched for any lookouts on top of the roofs of the surrounding buildings but he didn't spot anyone if they were up there.

He noticed a single, glass paned side door that led into the warehouse and he motioned for Hawkeye to follow him. Peering through the dirt crested pane, it was difficult to make out much, but Will finally spotted the black Cadillac like Jules had described. However, he didn't see anyone else inside.

"I think the place is deserted."

"Let me look." Hawkeye pulled him away from the window so he could examine the inside. He tried the handle on the door and it turned easy enough. "Stay close."

Will followed him inside, their revolvers drawn as they inched along a stack of old car tires. It made a good barrier wall hiding them from view, but also gave a good spy hole between the tires. He watched for a few seconds and noted that there was no movement on the other side of the barrier. Motioning with two fingers he gave the all clear for Hawkeye to continue forward.

"It's just like you suspected. This place is deserted except for the car," Hawkeye kicked on the tires.

"The GPS signal is still coming strong."

"That's because the phone is probably still in the trunk of the car."

"Or they left Jules and Eddie in there to suffocate." Will looked around the interior of the warehouse, followed the perimeter stairs up to the loft area and saw there was an office at one end, he pointed to it. "Look."

"Good eye. I missed it on first inspection. Better stay low to the ground not to draw attention from above. There should be a trunk release on the driver's side."

He nodded before bending low and scurrying across toward the car. Taking a moment, he checked inside to make sure no one was lying in wait before he slowly opened the driver's side door and pushed the trunk release.

A backdoor of the warehouse slowly slid opened and Will halted until he saw it was only TJ coming inside. He placed his index finger to his mouth and then motioned upward to indicate they thought the gang members might be upstairs. TJ nodded, stepped back outside and motioned for Harrison and O'Conner to follow him.

Will finally looked inside the trunk of the car and found it missing Jules and Eddie, but her cell-phone was tucked under a folded tarp. He retrieved it, disconnecting the call, checked for any hidden messages from her before he placed it securely in his top left cargo pocket. When he did that he noticed the left taillight was missing just like she said and there was a funny odor that he got a whiff of but couldn't place it, though it made him start coughing until he backed several feet away from the car.

"What's wrong?"

"Something in that trunk," he said, coughing again. He staggered, blinking several times and shook his head. "Whoa. For a second I thought I was going to pass out."

"Hey Burns." TJ motioned for him to come over to them. "There's a chemical in that trunk that almost took McLeod down. We may want to get a CSI unit to go over it if we take it into holding."

"If it almost took him down then it definitely took Gentry and the janitor out. Easy for moving them from one location to another." Hawkeye eyed Will. "How are you feeling? Do you think you can go on or should I call a bus to come check you out?"

"No. I'm fine."

"Are you sure?" Hawkeye asked again. "I don't want you going upstairs and having difficulty, or falling over the railing."

"I'm fine," Will stressed. "I'm not staying down here while the four of you go up there if there is a chance that Jules is being held up there. No little coughing fit is going to keep me down."

While he talked, he watched O'Conner and Harrison walk around the car inspecting it. They both began coughing like he did and moved away as fast as they could.

"There's a strong chemical odor coming from the car now," O'Conner said, putting his bend arm up in front of his mouth, coughing again, then clearing his throat.

Harrison bent over, placing his hands on his knees coughing deep, trying to clear his lungs.

"McLeod, what did you do to the car exactly?" TJ asked.

"Nothing but open the driver door and pop the

trunk so I could make sure that no one had been left inside."

"What if that was a trigger to release the chemical, like a booby trap?" TJ said.

"It may have been," Hawkeye agreed, coughing. "I think we need to get out of here."

"We can't, not when we aren't sure that Jules isn't upstairs in that office," Will reminded him, covering his mouth and nose with the back of his hand as the chemical smell became worse.

The car began smoking and flames shot from underneath it.

"No one is upstairs. It's a trap to make us believe they're here. Our CI set us up," Harrison said, running out the door.

O'Conner followed him.

Will took off toward the wooden stairs, but TJ and Hawkeye pulled him back with all their might.

"Don't be a fool, man," TJ said.

"They left the car and the phone here for us to find," Hawkeye said, guiding him out the door as the car became fully engulfed in flames.

Will walked backwards away from the warehouse, looking up toward the windows near the office, but he didn't see any movement. Jules' phone in his pocket started to ring and he quickly retrieved it.

"Hello?"

"Will?"

"Jules? Jules, where are you?"

"I don't have much time. I have a message for you. The chemical you inhaled will do to you what it did to the car if not treated. Tick tock."

"Wait, Jules!" The line was already dead before he got the words out. Her voice sounded shaky. He chalked it up to what she said being a ruse the gang was trying to use to prevent them from coming to look for her right away. But could they risk it?

He pulled the phone away from his ear and stared at it.

"What did she say?" Hawkeye asked. "Was she on the line long enough to get a location?"

Will shook his head. "No. They made sure she kept it short. She had a scripted message."

"What did they tell her to say?" Harrison asked, still having trouble with the coughing.

"That what we breathed in will cause the same damage it did to the car if we are not treated immediately. Tick tock."

"We'll begin to burn from the inside?" O'Conner asked.

Hawkeye coughed and shook his head, pointing in the distance. "To my cruiser. We're going to the nearest hospital to be checked out. We can't afford to take a chance that it's true."

WHILE THE CRUISER traveled to the nearest hospital

with lights and sirens blasting, Hawkeye called dispatch and had a firetruck sent to the warehouse address. Then he sent word to the police backup he'd already called for in the area to begin canvasing the Twin Cobras hangout locations looking for any signs of activity, but keep a low profile.

At the ER, the five were put into a curtained off area away from other patients so not to expose them to anything, and even the driver was examined to make sure he had not been contaminated. The doctor and nurses worked quickly checking their toxic levels to determine what they'd been exposed to so they could determine the best method of treatment. As soon as it was ruled out that pure oxygen wouldn't ignite or cause damage, each was given a mask to wear for optimal treatment.

Will never felt more helpless lying in the hospital bed with an IV needle stuck in his arm, flushing fluids into his system as he breathed in the oxygen. He needed to be out there combing the streets trying to find Jules. Precious time was slipping away from them. It had already been two hours or more since they arrived and team started working on them.

He couldn't believe that the Twin Cobras had gotten to her when he had felt the youth center was secure and under surveillance, but even that only worked to a certain extent. It didn't take into account when someone had a set of keys to the place, giving them access to offices and personnel. No one had seemed alarmed that Eddie was nowhere to be found today when Will asked if he'd been seen. For the day janitor no one paid much attention to his comings and goings, but maybe that's typical for a man in his position.

Will hit the bed with his balled fist but it didn't make him feel any better. The bed wasn't the problem; it was the waiting to learn if they could get out of here.

TJ, laying in the bed six feet away from him, pulled his oxygen mask down from his mouth. "Relax dude. You're causing your blood pressure to rise and we don't know what that might do to you. If it happens to you, we'll know it will happen to us and then we'll panic and it will be a chain reaction." TJ grimly smiled. "I've got a wife and little kids at home that are wondering where I am right now. Why I haven't come home to tuck them in tonight? And I can't call them until I know what to say. So who has it worse? You or me?"

Will pulled his mask off. "You, of course. All of you have lives outside of your jobs. I have nothing except my job, which is to protect Jules."

Well, that wasn't exactly true, he had Cassie, but she'd agree his job was his life.

Finally the doctor and his team of nurses

returned. The nurses went to work on unhooking the IVs while the doctor talked.

"I have good news. What you were exposed to was a strong irritant that made breathing difficult, but it isn't going to cause your body to combust like you were warned. I'm giving each of you samples of an anti-histamine that will help with the coughing. Take one tablet by mouth at night. If this doesn't help you can come back and see me here or go to your regular physician for a follow up."

"Any restrictions we should adhere to?" Hawkeye asked, sitting up on the side of the bed once the IV and oxygen mask were removed.

"I'd listen to your body and not overdo it. Some of you were exposed more than others, so your recovery time will not all be the same. Those with minimal exposure will bounce back quicker and those with more will take longer. Don't be shocked if you develop seasonal asthma after this exposure either. You may need to use an inhaler for a while."

"Where is the good news in all of this?" O'Conner asked. "Oh yes, we aren't going to catch on fire and burn to a crisp like a phoenix."

Harrison smacked his partner on the arm. "Stop being so flip. We're lucky we're walking out of here. Those punks could have barricaded the doors to the warehouse locking us inside. Did you ever think of that?"

"So doc," TJ said. "We're good? We can't expose

anyone we come in contact with once we leave here with this stuff, right?"

"You're clothes are questionable. That's why we are providing you with scrubs to wear out of here. Bathe as soon as you get home. Don't allow anyone else to touch your clothes since that could expose them to the chemical residue in the fibers, but once they're washed, everything should be good."

Will couldn't imagine being in Jules' apartment without her, but he would have to shower and change so he could go back out looking for her. He got his tactical bag from the cruiser before parting ways with Hawkeye and the others and headed to the closest 'L' line.

"Get some sleep tonight. We'll start looking again first thing in the morning," Hawkeye said.

"No. I'm looking tonight."

"Where?" Hawkeye asked before climbing into the cruiser.

"I'm going back to the youth center and watching footage of this afternoon and seeing if I see anything that sticks out to me. I'll call if I need back up."

"Fine. You do that."

CHAPTER 10

JULES SAT in the straight back chair with her arms tied behind her back and her ankles tied to the legs. She still had the sack over her head and she'd adjusted to breathing through it and keeping her eyes closed. Staring at the material so close to her face had made her feel claustrophobic. She'd lost track of time hours ago and had no idea where they'd taken her once they'd pulled her out of car trunk.

Poor Eddie. No telling where he was, but they'd taken him somewhere else after it sounded like they'd beaten on him for kicking out the taillight. It had been her fault – she'd told him to do it, but he hadn't said a word, protecting her.

At least they hadn't found her cellphone. Or had they?

They made her call it so she could talk to Will.

She didn't know how they knew he'd found it, but they did. And that message they made her read at gun point was creepy. She wondered what had happened to the Cadillac. It must have been pretty bad if they said the same would happen to him and the men he was with. She didn't like to think about what that meant. She refused to. She'd breathed in a funny smell while in the trunk and all it did was make it difficult for her to breathe and knocked her out. What if what they claimed would happen to Will would happen to her as well?

Rehashing all of this just made her antsy. It made her realize that she had been tied to this chair for a very long time and her neck was beginning to hurt, so was her back and her butt. She was tired and she wanted to lie down and go to sleep, but she didn't dare ask for anything. They'd given her a bottle of water earlier and a greasy hamburger from a gas station deli. It was what the one watching her was eating so she hadn't been afraid to eat it. Then he'd let her go to a windowless room with a toilet in it and a bare lightbulb for light. When she was finished, he led her back to what must have been the kitchen at one time and let her wash her hands at the sink.

"I'm not so bad," he said before shoving the sack back on her head and tying her up.

As for what she'd seen of her surroundings the place was nothing very descriptive. Just a run-down apartment, probably in a bad part of town. The few windows in the place had broken down cardboard boxes taped over them, which let little light inside, so bare-bulb lights were used to illuminate the rooms. There was no furniture and definitely no beds, so she could put that thought out of her head for sure. The only seating in the room where she was being kept was the chair where she sat and another squattier one that looked like it went with one of those kitchen dinette sets from the sixties. They were probably left behind when the last tenants moved out.

She thought for a moment about what would make it easier for her to get some sleep tonight and then how to get the guy to do what she wanted.

"Hey. Hey!" She yelled and waited to see if he came before she yelled again. "Hey!"

"What is it?"

"I'm not feeling so well. Is there any more bottled water?"

"No. There isn't. Just tap, but nothing to drink out of."

"Then could we move my chair over near the wall so I can lean against it? I really am not feel well. I think I'm going to be sick. I think if I could lean my head against the wall it would make me feel better."

"Listen, what do you think this is? The Shangri-

La and I'm your room service boy that you can make demands of like this?"

"I'm not making demands, I'm asking for a little help here. I'm not feeling well. I'd think you'd want to try to accommodate me so there isn't a mess to clean up. That's all. I think it was the hamburger. It was good, but a little too greasy for my stomach."

"Okay. Okay. I get it. I guess movin' your chair isn't that big a deal. I'll untie your ankles and lead you over to the wall."

"Thank you."

"You don't need to go back to the bathroom while we're at it do you? I don't want to have to come back in here again because you do." he asked, stooping to untie her ankles.

"No. I don't feel like I do."

"Now don't go thinkin' you can ask for a blanket because we don't got any."

"I'm fine with the sack over my head. It's keeping me warm."

"Okay, now let's stand and walk together."

He helped carry the chair over to the wall. The movement helped loosen the tightness in her arms and she noticed when he tied her ankles back they didn't feel as tight either. Then he did something she didn't expect, he untied her arms, let them fall down to her side and then looped the rope through them and secured them that way.

"No need for you to be so uncomfortable if you're feelin' sick."

"Thank you."

"In the morning it goes back before the others get here."

"Of course. I understand."

She listened carefully, making sure he was gone before she leaned her head against the wall and smiled to herself. It had worked better than she had anticipated. And the surprising part is she didn't feel guilty about it at all.

WILL LEFT JULES' apartment after he showered and changed and headed to the youth center, taking the 'L'. He was surprised to find a vigil outside of the center when he arrived. Hundreds of candles were lit, students as well as their parents, stood on the front walk all the way up and down outside where the trees lined. He was greeted by Clara who handed him a candle.

"Come join. We are doing this for Devon."

"He isn't dead?"

"No. No. The students are doing this in support of him. To show the gang that they haven't broken the students' spirits by what happened here today."

"Then no one has told you what happened to Jules," he said.

The woman blinked in the candlelight. "No, what happened?"

"She was abducted by the Twin Cobras outside in the back parking lot the afternoon. I've been trying to locate her all evening. I came back here to see if there was some clue that I missed."

"No. We had no idea. Should we disperse? Do you think we're in danger?"

"No. Stay. I think an outward show of community support is what is needed around here." Will gave her the candle back and walked up the walk, nodding and speaking to a few of the students he'd become acquainted with during the week.

When he got to the entrance, he took out his keys and unlocked the door, went inside and locked the door behind him, disarmed the alarm so it wouldn't go off and reset it before heading to his office. He'd stay there all night if he had to, watching footage from that afternoon until he was satisfied he'd not missed any detail leading up to and after Jules was thrown into the Cadillac. There had to be a piece of the puzzle that he'd missed.

Twenty minutes into the feed, he saw what he'd not known before. Jules hadn't been alone outside before the Cadillac pulled up. Why hadn't she told him? He refocused in on her sitting on the bench talking to Rodrigo, but they were too far away to make out what they were saying and he focused in on the teen when he got up and walked away. Jules followed him, stopping when Rodrigo did at the perfect spot for the Cadillac to drive by and snatch her on one side, while it looked like Eddie was being pulled from the other side of the car and tossed into the truck after she was put inside.

Once the car pulled away, Rodrigo sauntered back to the youth center as if nothing had happened.

Man that kid was cold. Two-faced and cold. He'd better not hear him say another word about how much he cared about Jules. It was clear he didn't care about anyone but himself.

Will tried to recall if he'd seen Rodrigo in the crowd of students at the vigil when he'd walked into the center. He wasn't sure, but there was one way to find out. He could go back out there and search the crowd, looking for him. If he wasn't, then he'd ask Clara to get him the kid's address and he'd go over to his place and make him tell him where the Twin Cobra's took Jules. Hell, he had half a mind to call Hawkeye and have a patrol unit go over to his place and have him arrested on aiding and abetting in the abduction of Jules Gentry.

Stalking down the hallway, back to the entry, he pressed the delay on the alarm so he could unlock the door and exit the building. He locked it back and joined the crowd. Troy, the teen from earlier, slapped him on the back when he stopped to stand beside him.

"Glad you could come out and join us."

"Me too. Have you seen Rodrigo tonight?" Will asked him.

"Yeah. He's with his parents about mid-ways up."

"Cool. I have a message from Jules for him. I'll see you." He moved to the perimeter of the crowd and searched slowly, not wanting to spook anyone.

It was like Rodrigo was waiting for him to reach their location. He spoke first. "Mr. Will, I want you to meet my Pops and Moms. This is Mr. Will. He's been with us this week, helping out at the center. He's the one I told you about that showed me all the cool basketball moves."

Will shook hands with his dad and mom.

"Where's Ms. Jules?" Rodrigo asked.

Will sucked in his breath, not believing the kid would actually ask that question. "That's what I'd like to ask you, since you were the last one to see her today. You know, before you allowed the Twin Cobras to snatch her from the back parking lot."

"Rodrigo!" His mother said. "No. My son isn't messed up with a gang. It would break my heart if he were. We raised a good boy. Sacrificed much to give him the best we can."

"Rodrigo." His father looked down at the ground. He didn't say anything more.

"Manuel?" the mother said to the father.

He reached for her and she hugged him, laying her head on his shoulder and began to cry.

"I was given a choice. A way out. They knew Ms. Jules trying to stop them from recruiting at the center. They wanted to stop her. They wanted to scare her a little that is all."

"So you gave her to them to save your skin?" Will said.

"You heard my Moms. It'd break her heart if I was involved with them. What else could I do? It was my chance to break clean with them. The only way they'd leave me alone."

Will shook his head. "Jules offered you help on several occasions, but you refused. I was working on an option to get you out and now the Twin Cobras have her and they have Eddie too."

"Eddie?" Rodrigo snickered. "They always had Eddie. He was a Cobra way back when he was a teen. That's why he wears that kerchief around his neck every day, so you don't see his Cobra tattoo. They pull him back in when they need him to do odd jobs. He's also the one who picks kids from the center for the Twin Cobras to recruit."

Son of a bitch!

The youth center administrators had no idea they had a traitor working among them, a man who talks as if he cares about the kids as much as Jules does. But in reality what he really cares about is finding the right kids to target for the Twin Cobras.

"For someone who isn't in the gang, you appear to know a lot."

Rodrigo shrugged. "Antonio tells me things. Maybe he talks too much."

"Did he tell you where they were taking Jules?" Will asked.

"No."

"Do you know anyway?"

"No."

"Would you tell me if you did?"

Rodrigo snickered and pointed a finger at him. "That's what I like about you, Mr. Will. You shoot straight. I don't know where they took her. Why would they tell me? I'm out. See, no bandana. No white kicks."

"Oh, and I thought Antonio gave you those for your birthday?"

"He did, but they had to go back to him. I severed all ties with them."

His mother wept harder and Will hated that he was causing her pain by questioning Rodrigo like this, but he had to get to the bottom of things.

"One more question. Do you have any idea where they *might* go – an off the beat location away from their normal hangout if they didn't want to be found?"

"There was this one place, an old warehouse

down near the waterfront in an abandoned part of town. It has double green doors and belonged to some of the first Cobras. A shell of a place really that they took me to once. I thought they were going to jump me and leave me there to die because I was holding out on agreeing to join, but instead, we stripped a car someone had stolen. The next day everyone got a cut of the profits on the sale except for me because I wasn't one of them."

"That place burned earlier tonight."

"Then I don't know where else they might have taken her. Obviously I wasn't in on as much as I thought."

"If she dies, don't think you can't be charged for helping them abduct her. I'll personally see to it that you do. You've talked about how you care about her so much and yet you handed her over to them without a thought."

"I'm a minor, what are they going to do, send me to juvie?"

His Pops smacked him on the back of the head.

Rodrigo's eyes widened and he swung around. "What gives Pops?"

"You don't speak to the man like that. He's trying to help you. Don't you see that? Tell him what he wants to know, Rodrigo. Tell him where they took, Ms. Jules."

"I honestly don't know. Why won't anyone believe me?"

The vigil crowd had dispersed and Troy had wandered over to where they stood. "What's this about Ms. Jules? Is she missing?"

The kid had a booming voice and others heard him say that. Students as well as their parents stopped and gathered around.

"Is it true? Is Ms. Jules missing?" Avril asked.

"Rodrigo? Did you have anything to do with this? I saw you talking to Ms. Jules this afternoon," Moni, another girl asked.

Rodrigo's basketball buddies huddled around him and when they were done talking to him in private, he came over to Will. "There might be one other place I hadn't thought of: 28 Dunston Street. It's an abandoned apartment building. The guys just reminded me of it as a place Antonio talked about going to play poker at sometimes. The place is empty but there is running water and electricity, so whoever owns it is still footing the utilities every month."

"I hope you aren't sending me on a wild goose chase."

"Honest. The boys remembered this. You can ask them."

Will looked over Rodrigo's shoulder where they were standing and they nodded at him. "I'll check it out. But you better keep your nose clean, kid. For your parent's sake if not your own. They deserve better."

Will made his way through the crowd and headed back toward the 'L'. He dialed Hawkeye's number on the way.

A groggy voice picked up on the other end. "Commander Burns here."

"Hawkeye. It's Will. I may have found her. I got an address out of the kid, Rodrigo, at the youth center. He said one of the Twin Cobras talked about it being a place where they sometimes meet up. It's an abandoned apartment building at 28 Dunston Street. It's a long shot, but the closest one I've found so far."

"Okay. I'll call for backup and I'll meet you there. Don't go in before I or backup arrives. You hear me?"

"I hear you." Will ended the call, but he knew that if he got there first he'd go in anyway.

DUNSTON STREET TURNED out to not be in a bad part of town. It wasn't anywhere you'd expect gang activity to be close at hand. He walked down the street, passed a few brownstones until he came to the eyesore number 28. It was a stucco that needed repainting bad and a streetlamp lit up the front like a beacon. The few shutters at the windows were hanging askew. It really looked like the place just needed some love and care with fresh paint and curb appeal and it would be as pretty as the brownstones. Whoever the owner was needed to step up and invest.

He was still standing there looking up at the place when Hawkeye arrived. "What are you staring at?"

"What could be a beautiful place to live."

Hawkeye chuckled. "It's an apartment building."

"It could be renovated to make each floor its own condo. There are four floors. I heard what you were talking to Hank about. You want us to head up a Brotherhood unit here. We'll need a place to live. That would give us each a floor to ourselves. And if there was a basement level we could set that up for storage."

"You're tired, Will. It sounds like a plan, but you'd need to talk it over with the others. Besides, is this place even for sale?" Hawkeye threw out.

"Semantics."

A patrol car drove past and parked a building away. The two policemen joined them about the time another team walked up as well.

"We're going in to search. We don't know if there is anyone inside, but we've been given a tip there might be someone being held in there. No shooting if we don't have to. We don't even know if the person is armed."

The six headed inside. The front door easily opened without squeaking. There was no elevator, so they took the open stairway that divided the main floor in two halves. Will went up, followed by Hawkeye. Two officers branched off to check the main level and the other two went downstairs. Will kept going up while Hawkeye stopped on the second floor.

Stopping on the third floor, he quietly walked down the hall, opening the apartment doors and going inside each one. He noticed that each window had cardboard boxes flattened and taped to the windows. The rooms were empty. Coming out of the first apartment, he left the door open so if the officers came up they'd know it had been searched. He checked the next and the next, until he got to the apartment on the backside of the building. He opened the door and went inside. There was a different feel about it than he'd noticed in the others he'd searched. The windows were still covered with the flattened cardboard boxes, but he saw a beam of light shining from down a hallway.

He stepped back out of the apartment and texted Hawkeye.

Third floor, apartment eight. There's a light on. I think this may be it.

Will went back inside the apartment and carefully walked toward the light. The hallway led to what once was a kitchen, where he saw a sleeping gang member slumped in a chair. He took a step toward an open doorway that had another light burning and thought it was empty at first, until he looked more closely. Leaning against the wall was Jules with a sack over her head.

He knelt in front of her and untied her ankles first. She didn't stir. Then he worked to undo her arms before he removed the sack from her head, gently raising her head from the wall enough to slip the sack over.

Hawkeye finally caught up to at that point. "You got her?"

"Yeah, but she's still asleep." Will stood and backed away. "Did you see the guy in the kitchen?"

"I didn't see anyone when I came in."

"No?" Will frowned. He stepped into the other room, but the chair was empty. Where could the gang member have gone? Just then a door opened and the gang member stepped out, but when he saw Will, he jumped back inside and slammed the door shut.

"He's in here!" Will called, rushing to the closed door and slamming his full weight against it, trying to break the door in. It took him kicking in the door to get the gang member out, but he was able to without injuring the guy.

Hawkeye and a groggy Jules finally came around the corner.

"How'd you ever find me?" she asked.

"We got a tip," Hawkeye said.

"You'll regret you ever messed with the Twin

Cobras," the gang member said. "You just wait and see what happens to her now."

"Shut your blabbering," Hawkeye warned, grabbing the guy by the arm and leading him out of the apartment. "Or I'll shut it for you."

Will looked at Jules. "You sure do make it difficult to keep you safe, you know that?"

"Oh, like I set out to have this happen?" she shot back.

"It's the company you keep. Mouthy teenage boys."

"Some of the girls can be just as mouthy."

"I haven't met any of them at your center that fit that description yet."

"That's because they're too busy swooning over you and your six pack."

He grinned. "Is that what it is?"

"Yep."

He stepped towards her and looked down at her. "It's been a long day, Ms. Gentry. I think you were right in wanting to stay at home. If I'd let you, then we would have avoided this horribly long day."

"Not on your life, McLeod. Poor Devon would have been beat up for nothing. Rodrigo wouldn't have gotten out of the gang. Some good has come out of it."

He shook his head. "I still don't see what good came from it when you count the hours you were tied up and had to wear that sack on your head, messing up your normally cute hair style. Now your hair is sticking up in every direction like you've been rolling around in the sheets doing all sorts of things."

She gasped and reached for her head with both hands. "Take that back. My hair will never look that way, even if I have been rolling around."

"I'll have to see it to believe it."

"Who says you'll be seeing it?"

He shrugged, reached for her hand, and entwined his fingers with hers. Then he leaned down and captured her lips with his mouth, giving her a searing kiss. When he pulled away, he nuzzled her neck near her ear and said huskily, "Promise me you won't ever put yourself in harm's way like that again."

"I can't make promises like that when I don't know what the future holds."

His phone buzzed and he swore under his breath before he answered. "Yeah, Hawkeye?"

"Do you want a lift back to her apartment? It's either that or catch a cab at this hour."

"Sure. We're coming down."

CHAPTER 11

JULES STRETCH dreamily and turned her alarm off again. She'd hit the snooze button several times already this morning. She didn't really want to get up and after the day and night she'd had, she felt she deserved to stay in bed longer. Hawkeye had wanted to give her and Will a ride to her apartment last night in order to debrief her about everything that had happened from the time she left her office with the Twin Cobra snakes, ran into Rodrigo and was snatched into the black Cadillac and so forth. As tired as she had been, she felt she had given him a very thorough run down of events.

The smell of fresh coffee greeted her and she finally made her eyes open more than a slit. She lifted her head up, but decided it felt too heavy to raise up so she stayed in bed and rolled onto her side.

A knock came at her door sometime later, startling her awake again. "Who is it?" she called, although she had a good idea it was Will.

"Room service."

"Didn't order any."

"Too bad. You're getting it." The door swung open with the last syllable and the fragrance of yummy food mingled with the coffee enticed her.

"I really am too tired to eat. I don't want to sound like a big baby, but can't you just let me sleep?"

"No I can't. This food has to be eaten by someone."

"You're more than kind to make me breakfast like this," she said.

"I didn't make it. Clara did. She came over before going to the youth center this morning. She said after what you had been through, you needed a hearty meal to get you back on the road to recovery."

"How'd she even know what happened to me?" Jules asked, finally sitting up. She scooted back toward the headboard so he could set the tray of food on her lap.

"Long story. The kids were holding a candlelight vigil for Devon at the center last night and I mentioned you had been taken and the others found out when I was interrogating Rodrigo about where the Twin Cobras might be hiding you."

"I see. Did she at least bring enough food so you could eat?" Jules asked him.

"She did."

"Good woman."

Jules dug in and realized she was ravenous. Or the food tasted so good she couldn't eat fast enough.

"Did they not feed you last night?"

"A greasy gas station hamburger."

"Not very appetizing."

"I pretended it made me sick so the guy would let me lean against the wall so I could sleep."

"Smart."

"Manipulative, but I didn't care. I was tied to a chair and being held against my will."

"Slow down or you *will* make yourself sick," he advised.

She took a drink of her coffee and tried to be slower as she ate the rest of the food, chewing more between bites. "Do I have to go anywhere today?"

"No. You can stay home. Unless you want to go somewhere later."

"Good." She finished off her plate and coffee, then Will took the tray from her. "Thank you."

"Get some rest."

She scooted back down in bed, lying curled up on her side, and hugged the extra pillow to her chest. Yawning, she closed her eyes and fell asleep within minutes, not waking up until after noon.

She took another shower when she woke up to help her feel better, even though she had taken one when she came in last night. Then she dressed in a pair of shorts and a t-shirt before going into the living room where she found Will on his laptop.

"You don't look that good. Are you sure you don't need more sleep?"

She walked over the kitchen and grabbed a bottle of water out of refrigerator and twisted the cap off. Taking a long drink, she finished off half the bottle. "I can't sleep anymore. I thought I'd veg out in front of the TV for a bit. Do you mind?"

"Go ahead."

She channel surfed for a bit, but all the local stations looked to be covering an incident that had happened, or was happening at Christ's Church today. "Will, look at this."

He closed his laptop and moved over to sit beside her on the couch from the armchair.

"What started out as a memorial service for the bartender that was killed in last Friday night's bar shooting has turned into chaos as gun shots peppered the parking lot and a car bomb went off here at Christ's Church on Hollandale. Chicago PD was already here in force paying their last respects, when this took place as mourners were leaving the church."

"Oh my God, there's Carly!" Jules watched as her friend was forced down to the ground by a man in a suit.

"That's my team leader Brand with her. She's protected by the best. He's the Devgru SEAL I was telling you about."

"But what were they doing there? Why would she be allowed to go to that funeral?"

Will started to answer her, but stopped when they both heard Hawkeye's voice on the TV.

"Chicago PD takes any act of violence against our citizens seriously and we are actively searching for the person or persons behind today's attack."

"So you do not believe this was connected to the shooting on Friday night, Commander Burns?"

"I cannot speculate one way or another until further investigation in the matter has been conducted. No one was gravely injured today and for that we are truly grateful."

"Thank you, Commander Burns."

"You see that. Hawkeye was at the funeral. He wouldn't have let Carly go if he hadn't felt it was safe for her to be there. There was no way he could have foreseen any of this happening, any more than we could have anticipated what happened to you yesterday."

"I still think it was too risky for her to have gone. She shouldn't have went."

A video clip of Carly and Brand escaping the SUV before it exploded flashed on the screen and Jules screamed, "See!"

"That does look bad. It's obvious that she is being targeted here."

Jules turned the TV off. "I can't take seeing anymore or the station rehashing what happened over and over. It's just gives whoever is behind this their five minutes of fame."

She drank the rest of the water and squashed the bottle in her hand. Then she turned to Will. "Do you think the Twin Cobras were behind that attack at the church? It did seem a little extreme compared to what they did to me."

"We got to you before they really had time to do anything to you. If we hadn't got Rodrigo to remember a possible location where the gang might have taken you, we wouldn't have located you last night."

"Rodrigo gave you the tip?"

"Yeah. After I confronted him in front of his parents at the vigil. He really didn't know where they took you, it was his friends that recalled the location that Antonio sometimes mentioned has a poker hangout."

"Poor kid."

"Don't feel sorry for him. He brought this on himself. Sure the gang targeted him, but he chose to get friendly with them and run around tasting what it would be like to be part of their crowd despite everything you and the other leaders at the youth center have been doing." Will shook his head.

"As for Eddie. I let Clara know his gang affiliation and she assured me he'd be let go today."

"Wait, what?"

"Eddie was a Cobra in his youth. He's been the one targeting the teens at the center for the Twin Cobras. Rodrigo told me all about him last night. So his being in the trunk with you was a ruse."

"Oh man. So they knew I had called you and that you knew the location of the car. I wasn't as clever as I thought. That means they didn't beat Eddie for breaking out the taillight, they only pretended to scare me for telling him to do it."

"So who was manipulating who?" Will asked.

"Ha ha."

A knock came at her apartment door and she froze. She rarely had visitors, especially during the day. And she wasn't expecting anyone, not when she couldn't see her friends.

"I hope you're hungry," Will said, getting up off the couch. "I ordered a pizza earlier."

She relaxed. "Of course I am. I think it's the post-trauma making me so famished."

She slowly got up and went over to the kitchen to get drinks out for them and plates. She met Will at the table and they ate thick crusted pizza with everything on it except the kitchen sink and anchovies.

"I didn't know what you liked, so I got a variety of veggies and meats."

"It's yummy," she said between bites. "You picked a good place to order from, too."

"You have their magnet on the side of the refrigerator, so I thought you must like the place."

She grinned as she ate. There wasn't much that got by him.

WILL TRIED CALLING BRAND, but the call rang and rang without being picked up. It didn't even go to voice mail. He sent him a text asking how things were with him and Carly, but he didn't get a response. This is how it had been all week and he was really beginning to worry that something wasn't right. He hadn't wanted to mention it to Hawkeye, but now he thought he needed to bring it up, especially after seeing what happened today at the funeral.

He took a long shot and tried texting Donovan to see if he got a response back from him. That was another one of his team mates he hadn't been able to make contact with this week. It could be nothing.

Then he sent a text to Wyatt to see how things were going with him and Colleen since they left town.

We're good. She's improving each day. Thanks for checking in. How are things your way?

Had a little trouble yesterday, but got it all

squared now. Nothing to upset Colleen with. Jules is fine.

That's good to hear. Over and out.

At least he was able to get in touch with Wyatt. He could let Jules know that Colleen was improving. That should lift her spirits. He'd tell her when she woke from her nap.

But then what? She'd want to know about Carly and he'd have nothing to tell her because he couldn't reach Brand. He texted Hawkeye, but got a response that he was unavailable because he was in a meeting. So that was that.

"What has you frowning so?" she asked, surprising him.

"That wasn't much of a nap."

"I didn't sleep. I couldn't. I just snuggled under the covers for a bit, but I never fell asleep. I thought about taking another hot shower, but that would be three since I returned home and I didn't think my skin could take it." She curled up beside him on the couch and laid her head on his shoulder. "Being home today is making me feel miserable. I wanted to be here yesterday and this morning, but now that I know what happened to Carly I feel like I need to be doing something other than waiting around here."

"Then what do you want to do? Go to the youth center to show the kids that you're okay?"

"I think so. Just for a little while."

"Then go change and we'll go."

THE YOUTH CENTER was abuzz when they entered. As soon as word spread that Jules was there, everyone came running to see her. The students circled her and the councilors stood back talking about how well she looked. Will stood off to the side with them, allowing Jules to mingle with the kids. Once she'd spoken to them, they moved away so others could reach her in an orderly fashion and Will was amazed with their behavior and knew that some adults could take a page out of their play book. Then he spotted Rodrigo and his basketball friends approaching. He watched them approach and wait their turn, but Jules didn't make a difference between him from the others. She hugged him and talked to him as if he hadn't traded her for his freedom the day before. She truly showed no malice toward the kid and Will couldn't understand it. Maybe she would have felt otherwise if things had turned out much differently and they had not gotten to her as soon as they had.

Once Rodrigo left Jules, he walked over to Will and offered him his hand. "I'm glad it all worked out and that you found Ms. Jules."

"Me too." Will shook his hand. "Thanks for the address."

"It was the guys more than me. They remembered it."

"Maybe we'll get to shoot hoops again sometime."

Rodrigo nodded and looked back at this friends. "We'd like that if you have the time."

Will's phone began to ring and he pulled it from his pocket, walking out of the youth center as he answered. "McLeod here."

"It's Hawkeye. You and Jules should come to the hospital. Brand has been hurt. He's asking for you."

"Hurt? How?"

"Just come. I've got to go."

Will put his phone back in his pocket and raked his fingers through his very short cut hair. His thoughts went back to the events shown on the TV earlier and he could only imagine what else might have happened. He hurried back inside the youth center and found Jules talking to her colleagues.

"I'm sorry to interrupt, but we have to go. That was Commander Burns. We're needed downtown."

"Downtown?" Jules questioned.

Will nodded. "We have to go."

"Go on," Clara said.

"Sorry. I'll see you next week." Jules waved as she hurried to keep up with Will as they left the building. They rushed down the tree lined walkway and reached the sidewalk leading to the 'L' in record time.

"Slow down, McLeod. Can you at least tell me what is going on now?"

"Hawkeye called letting me know that Brand had been hurt and he's asking for me and that we need to come to the hospital."

"What about Carly?"

"I don't know. He didn't say."

CHAPTER 12

A RED-FACED NURSE led Jules and Will down a corridor to what looked like a tucked away, private waiting room. She glanced back at them, but she finally pushed open the door a small way. "I'm sorry, Commander, but these people claim to know you. They refused to stay in the ER waiting area."

Jules could see Commander Burns stand and walk toward them and the open door. "It's alright. They can join us."

Behind him, she spotted Carly who stood up and sucked in a breath, before a smile spread across her worried face. Jules made a beeline to her friend, who she hadn't spoken to in almost a week. She could see tears pooling in Carly's eyes, and she blinked several times before Jules reached her for a tight hug.

"I've been so worried about you today, ever

since I saw the reports of the shooting at the church. Whatever made you go to the bartender's funeral? To risk your life like that?"

Carly pulled back and looked at Jules. "I was given the all clear to go. Besides I had to. You weren't there inside the bar when Phil was killed. Someone had to tell his wife how wonderful he was up to his last moments. If I'd been in her shoes, I know I'd have cherished having someone come to tell me that."

Jules hugged her again. *Yes you would have, Carly. It would have meant the world to you.*

"When we got the call tonight to come to the hospital," Jules said. "I knew it was about you. I never dreamed it was only about Will's friend."

"I've been worried about you too. Brand hasn't had a word from Will all week. We didn't know what was going on with you."

"What? I've texted him several times, but he hasn't responded. I thought it was because all I had to report was that things were under control. But you're saying he didn't get my texts?"

Carly shook her head. "He was really concerned yesterday when we headed to my job interview."

Jules touched Carly on her arm. "I wondered if you got to go. Did you get it?"

"No, but I was recommended to work with another designer to build up my portfolio and encouraged to apply again once I had."

"That sounds promising."

Carly nodded and took Jules's hand as she let it fall away from her arm, giving it a squeeze. "I'm so glad you're here."

"Me too. I think this has been the longest week of my life, not being able to get in touch with you."

The door to the waiting room opened and Carly dropped her hand as they turned to see who was coming into the private area.

"Carly! Jules!" Simone's squeal ricocheted around the waiting area as she entered the doorway, pulling Donovan behind her. Jules noted that he was as muscular and domineering-looking as Will, yet Simone had exerted her authority with him disregarding his orders and went to see Colleen at the hospital with Carly earlier in the week. The way Simone was leading him around today it looked like she had him wrapped around her finger and he didn't appear one ounce put out with her. In fact, he looked rather smitten.

"Oh. My. Gawd," a vaguely familiar voice said from across the room. "Simone Reid."

"Margot Wills!"

Jules turned not believing her eyes, surprised she hadn't noticed Margot sitting there when she first came in the waiting area. She watched as Simone and Margot met in the middle of the room and did the French kiss-kiss on each cheek that they did in college. Then she followed Margot's line of vision as the woman fixed her sight on Will and Donovan. She was surprised the barracuda wasn't licking her lips getting ready to pounce.

"Burnsie," Margot said, turning to the Commander, pointing to the men with her polished index finger. "Can you get me one of these?"

"Yeah, Commander Burns, she really needs one of these," Simone chimed in, "to keep her out of trouble."

"No. And double no. I should have known the two of you knew one another. You're too much alike."

Margot and Simone giggled, hugging one another. Linking arms, the two walked over to one of the two-seater chairs in the waiting area and sat down to talk.

Jules rolled her eyes, feeling as if this was more than she could handle. "How'd you run into Margot?"

Carly smiled. "It appears Commander Burns and Margot's father, the Senator, are acquainted. I had to move out of my apartment and needed a safe place to stay so I'm temporarily in the Senator's unused place on Lakeshore."

"Fancy."

"You can say that triple times." Carly crossed her arms and hugged herself. Jules noticed, but didn't say anything. She didn't know what had gone down with Carly this week, but now wasn't the time or the place to get into the details. She wasn't ready to reveal everything that had gone on with her either. They'd have plenty of time to catch up once this whole ordeal was over with and then she'd find out everything.

"Was Brand able to contact Will about what happened to Colleen? Were you notified about that?"

"We did get communication. Will and Wyatt have been able to text one another and she's doing well since leaving the hospital. That's all I know and all I want to know for her safety since she's moved to the safe house."

"How're the budget cuts at the youth center?"

"A donor stepped up at the last minute and saved us, again." Jules shook her head and sighed. "I hate these frantic periods. The kids at the youth center hate it because the staff is on edge and they can tell something is wrong. Will was a trooper. He saw me through it all. Did you know he's a fan of single-malt scotch?"

"That's great. I'm glad to hear your assigned protector has worked so well for you."

"What about Brand?" Jules asked, leaning in close. "How are things going for you? Have you gotten to use that leather teddy I gave you?"

Carly's face flushed. "No. How could you even ask me that with him lying in the ER?"

Jules smiled and shrugged her shoulders. "Curious to know if you'd had a chance to put it to use yet before this accident happened."

Carly stepped away from Jules and moved over to where the commander stood with Will and Donovan. Jules sat down close enough that she heard Will telling the commander about not being able to reach Brand all week.

"I haven't been able to since last Saturday either," Donovan said.

"I've had no trouble," the commander said. "Have either of you heard from Kincaid since then?"

They both nodded.

"I know for a fact that Brand hasn't heard from him either," Carly offered. "We discussed it on the way to my job interview. He was worried about all of his men because they'd been silent."

"Carly mentioned this when Jules and I arrived, so that's why I asked Donovan about it," Will said.

"Do you think someone has tampered with his phone?" Donovan asked.

The commander shook his head. "It's unlikely. He's been around very few people other than Kevin Petree and Carly all week."

"Don't forget Ragsdale," Carly said.

Commander Burns shifted his weight before saying, "But was Brand and the P.I. alone for any period of time for the man to have access to Brand's phone?"

Carly shook her head.

"What about Petree?" the commander asked. "Did you ever see Brand lay his phone down when Petree was around?"

"No, but I wasn't with them when Brand and Kevin went shopping for his suit. Kevin took him to the places he usually went and I stayed at the apartment. I can't imagine that he'd do anything to harm us. He's been so great all week."

"I'm not saying the man is guilty. I'm looking at the possibilities of who had access to Brand's phone. I'll get a tech guy down here to examine it and make sure it hasn't been tampered with so we will know for sure why the signals have been crossed."

Jules wondered who Ragsdale the PI and Kevin Petree were. She'd have to ask Carly about them later on. She got up and went to get a cup of water from the dispenser. When she returned, Carly had taken a seat, so she sat down beside her.

"What's wrong?" Jules asked, reaching for Carly's hand.

"Something the commander said about Brand's phone being tampered with. Only three people that could have done it. Our driver, the P.I. that Justin Porter hired to watch my apartment, and me."

"Justin did what? Is that who Ragsdale is?"

Carly nodded. "It's a long story and I'll tell you about it later. But, the most likely person to have messed with Brand's phone was our driver. I was trying to recall if I had somehow met him before, but I'm coming up with nothing."

"Why would the driver want to mess with an encrypted phone?"

"How do you know the phone is encrypted?"

"Will told me."

"So whoever messed with the phone would have to have a background in computer tech, wouldn't you think?"

"Yeah or hacking skills at least."

"I think that would rule out Ragsdale. He's a former detective, but I don't think he'd have the background in that."

"Your driver was a younger guy, I take it."

Carly nodded again. "Around our age. Just made detective. Doing his dues driving for the commander."

Jules sighed. "Maybe he resented being giving grunt work instead of a real case."

"But Brand has pulled him in to help protect me. He's not been *just* a driver. He's actually been involved in the last two days since the Twin Cobras broke into my apartment and trashed the place. Brand and Kevin have gotten all buddy-buddy with each other and that is a big step for my guy."

"Ah ha!"

The interruption came from across the space and Jules and Carly looked to see Margot pointing at Carly.

"So he is your guy."

"That was a figure of speech, Margot. Nothing more."

"Sure it was."

Jules turned away and rolled her eyes. That was so typical Margot. It was no wonder they never got along back in college. She bit her tongue and didn't say anything on the matter. It wasn't the time or place to squabble for Carly's sake. Her friend was worried enough about Brand and who could have tampered with his phone, putting them in danger.

Margot was a nuisance they didn't need to worry with right now. She understood why Carly was putting up with the woman since the Commander was having her and Brand stay at Senator Wills' apartment, but after this was over she prayed they could cut ties with her again.

It was late when Jules and Will returned to her apartment that night. She'd not wanted to leave Carly alone at the hospital, but the Commander had assured her that Carly and Margot would be going back to their apartments shortly. If she'd had her druthers, she'd have insisted on going home with Carly for the night, but she was certain that would've been out of the question.

She went straight to the kitchen and poured two single-malts. Will followed her and she handed one to him before clinking her glass with his. "Here's to the end of a rotten day."

"Here's to getting to see your friends and mine. Even if not under the best of circumstances."

She downed the scotch and felt guilty for thinking about the bad while he thought of the positive.

Discarding her empty glass on the counter, she placed a hand in the center of his chest, feeling the beat of his heart underneath her palm. The natural need she felt growing for him stemmed from knowing he was close by, but that was all it was, right? Sure, he'd kissed her twice now, but that didn't mean anything did it? She patted the spot a couple of times before dropping her hand and walking to her bedroom. "Good night."

"Good night, Jules."

WILL POURED another splash of scotch and put the bottle back in the cabinet. He leaned against the counter and drank the liquid, feeling as out of sorts as he suspected Jules did with the way she'd left the kitchen. When he finished his drink, he sat the empty glasses in the sink and ran water in them before turning out the light and heading to his room. He took a quick shower then settled in bed. But sleep wasn't coming.

He tossed and turned for a bit, then he heard footsteps in the hallway approaching his door, so he wasn't surprised when it slowly opened.

"Will, are you asleep?"

"No. You having trouble, too?"

"Yes."

"Want to talk about it?"

"What's to talk about?"

"Why we can't sleep."

"You think it was the scotch?"

"No, smarty. I don't think it was the scotch. That should have relaxed us."

"But it didn't."

"The opposite. It made me cagey." He sat up in bed, the springs moaning with the shift of his weight. He flipped on the bedside lamp so he could see her better.

She stood in the doorway, holding onto the doorframe as if she needed support. The almost snug nightshirt she wore that hugged her curves and left little to the imagination, fell just above her knees. He silently groaned.

"What are we going to do about it?"

"Getting hot and sweaty has always worked for me."

"That depends on how you plan to get hot and

sweaty," she said, her eyes growing larger as he walked toward her.

"Exercise of course. Is the gym open downstairs?"

"No. I-I don't know." She sounded really flustered by the question.

"Unless you have a better idea?" he asked, titling her chin so she was forced to look up at him.

Her eyes had already dilated and her breathing had quickened from his simple touch. She'd come to his room for one reason, even if she wasn't willing to admit it. She'd been unable to admit it when she'd laid her hand on his chest in the kitchen before she left him to go to bed. He'd just not picked up on the signal quick enough or they could have avoided this awkwardness.

She never imagined she'd be the girl to want him to make the first move, but she did. She wanted to know that he wanted her as much as she was wanting him right now.

Her lips parted and she licked her lips with the tip of her tongue inviting him to do the same. Taking her invite a step further, she leaned in a little closer and ran her hands up his arms.

"I like your idea better," he said.

"But I didn't say anything," she breathed.

"Your eyes spoke volumes," he whispered, leaning close to her ear. He began kissing her neck with tiny kisses, feeling her swallow several times as he moved around to the dip in her collarbone. She leaned her head back, exposing her neck to him as she moved her arms around his neck. He picked her up, forcing her to straddle his waist as he carried her over to his bed.

"What's your preference, top or bottom?"

"Do you always ask?"

"No, but since you don't always tell me what you want, I thought I'd save you the trouble."

"I think I've been pretty forth coming since you kissed me the first time."

"Not true."

"I'll take the bottom for now."

"Good choice. You won't be sorry."

JULES GIGGLED SINKING DEEPER into the mattress as he laid down with her and they started kissing. For the first time in several days she wasn't worried about her friends, the youth center, or the Twin Cobras gang. All she could think about was how wonderful it felt to be in Will's arms and how she never wanted to be anywhere else. She didn't know where tonight was going to take them, but she was happy for now and she'd settle for it.

EPILOGUE

Two weeks later...

Jules closed the manila file folder and opened her desk drawer to put it away when a knock came at her door. She looked up, surprised to see Commander Burns. "Hawkeye! What brings you down to the youth center?"

"Can I come in?" he asked, pointing at her guest chair.

She stood and held out her hand, motioning toward the chairs in front of her desk. "Of course, take a seat. Should I call Will?"

"He's on his way. I already let him know I'm here." Hawkeye smiled. "You're looking better than the last time we met."

Jules thought back to when that was and

remembered it was the night Brand was in the ER. "Gosh, after the twenty-four hours you'd had with my abduction and then the Christ's Church chaos, I'm surprised we weren't all looking ragged."

"True."

"Do you know when my life will be able to go back to normal? I'm not complaining about Will being my protector. I've gotten accustomed to that, but surely I can start going about my business without having to worry someone is out to get me, can't I?"

"Actually, that's what I'm here to talk to you about."

Will came in and pulled her office door closed behind him. "Sorry. I was held up in the hallway."

"No problem. What I came to tell you both is that we finally caught the Twin Cobras that were part of the kidnapping. We got Eddie right away when he reported to work the next day, but these guys were harder to track down."

"Too bad you can't get all of the Twin Cobras off the street," Jules said. "That's what this area needs. One less gang in town."

"I agree with you totally there, but can you be happy to know that six of them are off the street now. The one we took in custody the night we found you, Eddie, and then four others. We charged them with burning the warehouse too, so they should be sentenced with six to twelve months in jail for that alone."

"What about the Christ's Church attack?" Jules asked. "Did you determine if the Twin Cobras were involved with that as well?"

"No. I'm afraid the gang had nothing to do with it. In fact, the gang member we had in custody from the bar shooting was killed that morning in his cell. The pieces of the puzzle didn't fit together at first, but we soon figured out who was behind it all. Kevin Petree, the young detective I'd taken into driver's pool and assigned to Brand and Carly. He was working with Carly's ex-husband and he was responsible for what happened at Christ's Church and other crimes."

"Someone needs to lock Justin Porter up."

"He has been arrested and is facing criminal charges now."

"I bet Carly is thrilled by that news," Jules said.

"I have one question, if the gang member you had in custody from the bar shooting was killed, then Jules is no longer needed to testify in the murder trial, is she?" Will asked.

"No, she isn't. Unfortunate for the bartender's wife that no one will be charged for her husband's murder."

"Then my services here are no longer needed?" Will asked.

"Not so fast. The Twin Cobras are still a threat

to the youth center. They may still try to come after Ms. Gentry. We hope not, but until the center can budget in someone to serve as their security person, I'd like you to stay put if you don't mind."

"Certainly. I just needed to know what you wanted me to do."

"This is your first official role as a member of the new Chicago Protection Task Force."

"So you got the funding?" Will asked.

"I did."

"As for me, I want to know can I see my friends again."

"You may."

"Excellent!" Jules reached for her cellphone.

"What are you doing?" Will asked.

"Calling Carly and Simone. We're so overdue for a girl's night."

"Heaven help Chicago," Hawkeye said, getting up to leave.

ABOUT LEANNE TYLER

Award-winning author Leanne Tyler writes sweet and somewhat sensual romances whether historical, contemporary, or romantic suspense. Her newest series the Chicago Protection Task Force is part of the Brotherhood Protection World. Other series includes her popular The Good Luck series-- a collection of short contemporary romantic comedy romances set in East Tennessee. In addition to her contemporary novels, she writes American historical novels set prior to and during the Civil War.

Leanne lives in East Tennessee with her son. For more information about her books and to sign up for her newsletter, please visit leannetyler.com.

BROTHERHOOD PROTECTORS

ORIGINAL SERIES BY ELLE JAMES

Brotherhood Protectors Series

Montana SEAL (#1)

Bride Protector SEAL (#2)

Montana D-Force (#3)

Cowboy D-Force (#4)

Montana Ranger (#5)

Montana Dog Soldier (#6)

Montana SEAL Daddy (#7)

Montana Ranger's Wedding Vow (#8)

Montana SEAL Undercover Daddy (#9)

Cape Cod SEAL Rescue (#10)

Montana SEAL Friendly Fire (#11)

Montana SEAL's Mail-Order Bride (#12)

SEAL Justice (#13)

Ranger Creed (#14)

Delta Force Rescue (#15)

Montana Rescue (Sleeper SEAL)

Hot SEAL Salty Dog (SEALs in Paradise)

Hot SEAL Hawaiian Nights (SEALs in Paradise)

Hot SEAL Bachelor Party (SEALs in Paradise)

ABOUT ELLE JAMES

ELLE JAMES also writing as MYLA JACKSON is a *New York Times* and *USA Today* Bestselling author of books including cowboys, intrigues and paranormal adventures that keep her readers on the edges of their seats. With over eighty works in a variety of sub-genres and lengths she has published with Harlequin, Samhain, Ellora's Cave, Kensington, Cleis Press, and Avon. When she's not at her computer, she's traveling, snow skiing, boating, or riding her ATV, dreaming up new stories. Learn more about Elle James at www.ellejames.com

Website | Facebook | Twitter | GoodReads | Newsletter | BookBub | Amazon

Follow Elle!
www.ellejames.com
ellejames@ellejames.com

facebook.com/ellejamesauthor
twitter.com/ElleJamesAuthor